Heroes Die Young

T. M. Hunter

For Elias,

Second Edition

ISBN: 978-1-50272-339-0

Dedication

For Cheryl, who constantly makes me feel like a hero.

Other Titles from T. M. Hunter

Friends in Deed

Death Brings Victory

The Cure

Seeker

Dead or Alive: An Aston West Collection

Chapter One

I awoke to a seductive female voice. "Aston…"

Too bad for me, it belonged to Jeanie, my ship's computer. A cruel joke, designed mostly for male pilots traveling long distances alone. It was even worse when I ignored the fact she was simply a machine, programmed to think.

I grumbled, "What?"

"We're entering the Toris system."

I sat up from the hard, low-lying bunk, stood and walked toward the front end of my ship. My hope was that Toris would be my gateway to temporary financial security. It was a short distance, nonetheless painful, as metallic floor panels clanked under my feet louder than normal.

As I walked onto my bridge, the hyperspeed engines disengaged and slowly wound down. I held onto my captain's chair to steady myself until we reached a constant velocity.

I sat down in my chair, stuck my hand into the side pocket, and grabbed the same bottle which put me down after our last stop. "How are we doing on time?"

"Far ahead of schedule."

In the second of my four cargo hatches was a cargo container full of blue organic crystals. When I'd picked it up, the seller had instructed me to take it to Toris, the outer planet in the system of the same name. I hadn't been told why they were needed so quickly, but he'd said I'd double my pay if I made it to Toris ahead of schedule. I didn't need to be told twice.

"Let me know when we reach the station."

I took a small taste of the light yellow liquid in the bottle. The Vladirian storekeeper peddling the stuff at my last stop had given me the full story behind the drink. An animal native to Vladiria, a small passive thing called a Roshtu, would secrete the liquid as a defensive measure when attacked. The sweet smell and taste of the liquid would cause the attacking predator to concentrate on lapping up the liquid, intoxicating it and allowing the Roshtu to escape unharmed.

I took another drink, this one longer. It was a dangerous combination of tasty and addictive. I had to wonder if those predators ever woke up feeling like this. "So, what would you like me to buy for you once I get paid?"

"I am currently running at peak performance, and have no requirements."

I smiled and leaned back in my chair. I usually found scuttled and abandoned cargo, then sold it for profit. Scavenging was a less aggressive form of piracy, and usually safer, since you didn't have to carry out threats of violence. Unfortunately, such cargo tended to be scarce, and had been more so lately. So, when I'd stumbled into an opportunity to carry cargo, I jumped at the chance. An extra bonus for speedy delivery didn't hurt matters.

I took another sip of the Vladirian liquor and put it away. There needed to be something left to celebrate my newfound fortune with. "ETA?"

She ignored my question. "I'm picking up a ship on medium range sensors."

The hairs on the back of my neck rose. "Show me."

My viewscreen lit up along the front wall of my bridge. A couple of kilpars in length, the lines of the ship were smooth, tapering from the nose to a constant rectangular cross-section around the first quarter of the hull. Near the back of the ship, I could see bell-shaped nozzles behind four embedded engines, darkened against the starfield. I recognized the configuration, but wanted confirmation. "Rulusian freighter?"

"Designation Green Three."

I took another look at the sensor screen beside my left armrest. "I don't see any other ships out there."

"There are none in the vicinity."

A Rulusian freighter in an alien system, all by itself, made no sense. They often stuck together in vast convoys, to give themselves a better defensive position through sheer numbers.

"Status of the freighter?"

"Engines and main power are down, backup systems are in effect. No shields, no weapons charged." She paused a moment. "No life signs."

With the condition of the ship, and no crew, I wondered what happened. Then a smile crossed my lips. I was a scavenger pirate at heart and wasn't about to let a prime opportunity escape. "Any cargo in the bays?"

Jeanie was hesitant. "Yes."

"Well," I chuckled, "what is it?"

"Signs of cargo without accompanying records in the transport manifest."

Contraband. My smile grew. Rulusians were usually law-abiding as well. I had no idea why one of their ships would be hauling illegal cargo, but with three open bays on my ship and plenty of time to spare, there was only one thing on my mind.

Jeanie was too smart for her own good. "The logic of this situation does not compute."

"It's nice you worry about me, but I'll be fine." I smirked at the thought of a machine having feelings.

She remained silent.

"Access their computer, and drop their cargo."

"Unable to comply."

If she wasn't programmed to obey, I would have been upset. There had to be something wrong. "Explain."

"The on-board systems were placed under a command-level lock-out by the Captain of the vessel. Only the Captain can remove it."

I clasped my hands behind my head and sighed. Green Three grew larger in the viewscreen as we approached it. Finding the freighter made me think my luck was turning for the better. Now, the situation was tougher than it first seemed.

My thoughts drifted to the state of the ship. "Looks like they didn't want anyone else gaining control. Maybe they abandoned ship."

"That theory appears plausible."

I ran my hands through my dark brown, wavy locks, then massaged the tension out of the back of my neck. "I guess I'll just have to go over and drop it manually. Move us to the starboard docking hatch."

• • •

Soon, I stood inside the airlock compartment of the Rulusian freighter, my Mark II blaster in my right hand. A crude and stubby weapon, it was small enough to hold with just the one hand, with a recoil guard propped against my arm. It had always been there for me, and never let me down. Hopefully I wouldn't have to put that streak to the test.

I lifted the left sleeve of my black leather jacket up and spoke through the embedded transmitter. "Can you get me through the airlock hatch?"

"Negative."

Green indicator lights above the inner circular hatch told me the pressures had already equalized. I stooped over to the left and looked at my reflection in a dark computer screen mounted in the wall. My face was rugged, covered with a few lines and weathered by experience. My once bright blue eyes were dim from the passage of time. I quickly grew tired of looking at myself and yanked the screen from the wall. It dangled from a large jumble of wires.

It was a mystery which ones controlled the locking mechanism, so to save time, I ripped all of them out amidst snapping sparks and rancid fumes. The screen dropped to the floor and smashed. The door popped loose, just enough where I could put my fingers around the edge. The muscles in my arms bulged slightly as I strained. Finally, the door hit a point where it rolled out of the way on its own and I ducked through the entryway.

"I'm in," I announced to Jeanie, out of breath.

"Be careful."

Inside, I broke into a sweat, both from the physical exertion and the climate controls on-board the freighter. Rulusians were from an extremely warm and humid jungle planet, and liked to make their ships feel like home. My heavy jacket didn't help matters. Lines of sweat made their way down my face, as I stepped away from the airlock hatch.

I turned my gaze down the entry corridor and saw carnage I wouldn't soon forget. Rulusian bodies were piled on either side of the hallway, burn marks from energy weapons appearing as black patches on their dark green skin. The putrid scent of scorched flesh was in the air. I passed an open doorway on my left, and looked inside at crew quarters. More Rulusian corpses lay amidst sparks and clouds of smoke.

I lifted the transmitter again. "You're sure there isn't anyone on this ship?"

"Affirmative. All scans show nothing but yourself."

"This damage is far too recent."

"Did the crew abandon ship as we had thought?"

I grimaced. "Doesn't look like it."

I continued down the corridor toward the bridge. Smoke particles lingered in the air and I detected a faint chemical odor while my eyes watered. Dark blast marks lined the doorframe and floor, where an access hatch had been blown open with some sort of bomb. I took slow, cautious steps through the opening and became witness to even more carnage. Ten more Rulusians had collapsed against the outer wall or slumped over consoles, all roasted by weapons fire. I definitely didn't need to meet up with the people who had done this. I didn't get into the scavenging business to be a hero. Everyone loves heroes, but heroes have a tendency to die young.

I glanced at the console screens while stepping around the short end of an oval-shaped half-wall. All of the displays flickered with minimal power from backup systems, while I stepped over a pair of corpses. I stopped at one and attempted to bypass the lockout. The sweat fell off my face onto the screens and formed little pools which slowly worked up enough courage to slide down the panel. I realized my attempts were useless and walked to a single access hatch at the back of the bridge.

"Jeanie, which bays contain contraband?"

"All of them."

A huge smile spanned my face. This was definitely a dream come true.

Unfortunately, I only had three bays open and there was no way I was dumping the crystals. Perfect opportunities like these were the exception and after these weapons were sold, I'd likely have to run some more regular cargo. Even in such a huge universe, it wouldn't take long for word to spread that I couldn't be trusted to complete a delivery.

"Get ready to pull three containers in. The winches should be adequate." I had a loading arm installed, and even though it was a lot more accurate, it was slow and cumbersome. There was still a bonus on those crystals to keep in mind.

"Acknowledged."

The door into the cargo hold slid open easily, which I found odd as I walked inside. The air was stale and dry in my lungs as the floor panels clanged and echoed with each step. The door closed behind me and I glanced down the dimly lit corridor at six bays on either side. The best thing would be for me to drop the first three bays and ignore the possibility of a better catch in the others.

A computer console beside the bay door monitored the ambient conditions inside, while a marked service panel underneath drew my attention. I shoved my Mark II into its holster inside my jacket and knelt beside the panel. The cover pried off in no time and I tossed it aside. A lever on the right, and two dimmed lights next to it looked like what I needed. Even though I'd never jettisoned cargo manually from a Rulusian freighter before, there were plenty of bays left to find the proper technique. After I pulled the lever, the lights flashed in an alternating sequence, rapidly increasing in speed before they turned solid. A miniature explosion sounded off as the bay evacuated itself.

Just to make sure I hadn't destroyed a perfectly good cargo container, I lifted my transmitter again. "Do you see it, Jeanie?"

"Pulling in the cargo now."

"Two more on the way."

I moved on to the other bays, going through the same process. As the third bay jettisoned, I heard a metallic clang echo farther down the hold.

I pulled out my Mark II and stood, as a woman with bronze skin and black hair jumped out from a crawlspace under the floor. She raised a disintegrator cannon and pointed it at me. I dropped to the floor just before her first shot hit the bridge door behind me and showered sparks down onto the floor grills. I fired a three-shot burst and she dropped down in the crawlspace again, while minimal damage was done to the aft bulkhead. At least it gave me the opportunity to run toward the bridge door, where the impact mark from her first shot still glowed. Eager for cover, I ducked into a small alcove at the front of the hold as another shot struck the wall. Sparks fell at my feet while I pressed my back firm against the cold hard metal. My heart beat faster than it had in quite a while.

I yelled out, "You can have the rest. I've got all I can carry." I had no idea how this person evaded Jeanie's scans, but my main concern now was to get out of this alive.

"This is my ship, idiot." Her footsteps drew closer.

"Funny, you don't look Rulusian." I eased my head out and quickly jerked back as another shot hit the corner. More sparks showered the grating at my feet.

"Come on out. You can't escape."

"And get myself shot? No thanks." The blaster felt loose in my hand, while my palms grew damp.

"Slide your weapon out first."

I had no choice. Disintegrator cannons were outlawed for civilian use almost everywhere, and for good reason. "Okay, okay. I'm coming out." I slid the blaster along the grill and lifted both hands high in the air.

She taunted me as I walked out to face her. "You board ships, and arm yourself with a toy?"

I didn't care for her insults, but wasn't in a position to complain. "I didn't expect visitors."

"Glad to see some old tricks still work." She smirked.

Jeanie's voice was frantic over my transmitter. "Aston, Aston!"

A little late, I thought. I looked at my captor with an edge to my voice. "Mind if I take this?"

She scowled and grabbed her weapon a little tighter.

"My ship's computer," I told her.

She gave a stern nod and I held my wrist over to my mouth. "What is it, Jeanie?"

"A pair of attack cruisers are on an intercept course from Toris."

My captor relaxed her grip on the cannon. "You're not part of a boarding crew?"

"I'm just a scavenger pirate." I reached down for my blaster. "We need to go."

She was loud and abrupt. "Hold it."

I looked up, the barrel still pointed at my face.

I frowned. "Come on. We don't have time for this!"

"How can I trust you? You're a thief."

I let the insult slide. "Right now, it doesn't look like you have a choice. You can stay here and wait for those attack cruisers to show up if you want. Me personally, I plan to be on a ship that can run." I grabbed my blaster and stood.

The reality of her situation finally sunk in. "Okay, let's go."

"Finally," I muttered as we ran back toward the docking port.

Chapter Two

I shoved my Mark II blaster into its holster and plopped down in my Captain's chair as Jeanie gave us an update. "The cruisers are approaching weapons range."

Our guest sat down in the co-pilot's seat, and stared at the viewscreen with bitter anger. My ship's airlock disengaged from the freighter with a loud clunk while my attention was on the sensor screen to my left. It wouldn't be long until those cruisers were right on top of us.

"Get us out of here, Jeanie. Pump up the background noise." The larger sensor reading of the Rulusian freighter should have been enough to shield us from view. At least I hoped so, because my ship wouldn't last long against two warships.

The woman kept her gaze on the viewscreen. "Background noise?"

The impulse jets fired, a muffled sequences of hisses coming from all around us. Then the aft engines lit off for a few moments to gain some distance from the freighter. "We alter our emitted radiation levels so they can't tell us from the rest of space."

"As long as they don't have windows."

I shrugged and looked at the weapon controls panel, centered between the two chairs. My proton cannons were fully charged, but there were only two rockets in my weapons bay. Being outnumbered and outgunned was not my idea of a good time, so this plan needed to work.

I checked with Jeanie. "Is it working?"

"The cruisers are within weapons range."

And we were still in one piece, which was good news for a change.

"Zoom in."

Jeanie obeyed and I saw both cruisers and the freighter clearly.

The Torian cruisers were small for their class, about a quarter kilpar long, and elliptical, with two engine pods mounted awkwardly around the aft quarter of the ship, a true testament to non-aesthetic design. Though they looked ugly, I was certain they didn't lack in functionality.

They broke off into a side-by-side formation and gained speed while we watched. Jeanie gave us a play-by-play account. "The cruisers' weapons arrays are on-line. They are commencing their attack run."

I watched while the two jetted along the length of the freighter, firing at will. Energy beams and projectiles struck all sections of the derelict ship. They made no move to try and board the vessel, their sole intent being its destruction. I glanced at my reluctant traveling companion out of the corner of my eye. The freighter went through a slow, merciless death, before the failing structure finally collapsed and imploded. She flinched as if she was being killed herself.

Debris floated away from the scene of the crime as the cruisers made wide turns and headed back toward the distant planet. Their assault on a defenseless, and mostly crewless, ship had been little more than a training exercise for any semi-competent attackers.

I turned to our guest and noticed the red jumpsuit which clung to her body. "I guess you'll be coming with us." She said nothing as I offered my hand and continued, "Aston West."

She spoke bitterly and didn't bother with the social niceties. "Rione Sc'lari."

"So, for my own benefit, can you tell me what you were doing with so much illegal cargo on-board?" My gaze fell upon the disintegrator cannon in her lap and a new uneasiness set in.

"No." Her head whipped around, sinister green eyes burning into me as her long black hair swung out of place. Small ridges were revealed on the left side of her face. I'd never seen such a thing and was intrigued, despite the fact she'd just tried to kill me.

One large ridge covered the skin in front of her ear, while smaller branches shot off in all directions. All of them were a deep red color, which I figured was a sign she was angry. I hardly needed the hint.

She quickly pulled her hair back in place. "What I was doing with my ship is none of your business."

"How about who massacred your entire crew?"

She continued her silent treatment.

"Why would those Torian cruisers exert the effort to destroy your ship? I would think they'd at least confiscate your cargo."

She stared at the viewscreen without comment. I sighed and shook my head. "Jeanie, resume course. I'll be back in the cargo hold doing a quick inventory."

Rione stood and cut me off as she walked back to the living quarters. This entire situation was more than I had bargained for already, so I planned to have a look through this newfound cargo myself and not bother trying to get answers from her. That was a lost cause from what I'd seen so far.

She took a seat at the small round table opposite my cot and glared at me while I walked toward the hold. "You won't get away with this," she hissed.

"Strange way to treat a person who just saved your life."

She turned to look away as the cargo hold hatch opened. The floor panels echoed under my feet when I stepped inside.

"Make sure I'm not interrupted," I instructed Jeanie. "Once those cruisers are out of range, shut down the noise generators and resume course." Even with this latest excitement, I was still on-track to get my bonus, but didn't want to chance something else happening along the way.

"Acknowledged."

The hatch closed behind me and the small corridor was bathed in dim lighting from above. I stepped over to the left and used the keypad, located to the right of the first bay's hatch, to open it. The round door creaked its objection as it slid aside and I walked in.

Unlike the corridor, the bay was lit up bright as day. I rubbed my hands together to warm them and watched fogs of breath exit my mouth. Unfortunately, the heating system hadn't had time to bring the bay's temperature up to normal.

"Let's see what we have here." I took two steps over to a rectangular container which nearly filled the bay and came up to my shoulders. Two sets of levers rotated down from the corners, which allowed me to push open the lid. I climbed up on the cargo bay's support structure and took a peek inside.

I about fell to the floor when I saw racks of illegal weapons stacked as tight as they could be. This container alone would set me up financially for a long time. I shivered from the cold and from the sheer fact of my good fortune, then quickly dropped back to the floor and went about the business of re-latching the container. I felt the aft engines through the ship's vibrations, and knew we were continuing our journey.

The other two bays contained the same cargo in the same quantities. Fate had finally smiled on me, and I was giddy with excitement.

As I walked back out of the hold, Rione still sat at my table. Her stare was blank and she almost looked as if she was sleeping with her eyes open. I decided not to start another argument, and continued toward the cockpit without incident.

Now I just needed to decide what I would do with all the money I stood to make.

• • •

The remainder of the trip was thankfully quiet and uneventful. There was no sign of the Torian cruisers as we approached the orbital station. I gazed at the planet in the background. Its bluish-white surface radiated brightly, even though it was farthest from the star at the center of the system.

I broke free of my near-trance and thought of the extra cargo I had on-board. "Shield the cargo, Jeanie."

"I've had it shielded since we left the Rulusian freighter."

"Always one step ahead of me. Let's just hope it works."

"It will."

A message erupted through my speakers, "You have entered Torian space. Please identify yourself."

I recited the galactic code that identified my ship. "Sierra-Tango-Four-Two-Four."

There was a long pause, much longer than it should have been. I wondered if something had been placed on my ship's records without my knowledge, or if it was simply a case of overzealous and paranoid locals.

Fortunately, the response came back before I had to make any kind of drastic decision and run for my life. "Please proceed to docking ring two, port thirteen. Transmitting the coordinates."

"Acknowledged."

Jeanie guided us in as I took in the sight of the station itself. The outside of the station was grim, dark, and took up most of the viewscreen. Six rectangular walkways connected three concentric rings like spokes as they ran to a central hub. A large boom reached for the planet from the center of the hub.

I hadn't been given any specific location for the meeting, with the buyer's intermediary telling me that they would find me. That central hub seemed as good a starting point as any. The station loomed ever closer as Jeanie did her usual expert job of navigation. We approached the middle docking ring and lights flashed next to the port we were destined for.

The ship bumped against the port and the docking clamps gently hissed as they engaged.

I announced my intentions to Jeanie, "After we dock, I'll meet the buyer. Once the money's transferred, we're leaving. I'd rather not spend more time here than I have to."

"Understood."

"I'll need to find out the protocol for the cargo transfer."

"I have already begun transfer of the crystals to this port's cargo bay. According to the station's computer, the bay can be accessed via a computer terminal. There should be one next to the airlock after you enter the station."

"What would I do without you?" I stood from my chair.

"Live your life a hollow shell of a man."

I chuckled and started out of the room. Before I made it through the doorway, Jeanie continued, "You'll have to pick up a cargo storage pass in order to sell the merchandise."

Rione leaned against the airlock hatch, primed and ready to leave as soon as the pressure equalized. I looked over in the far corner where she had left the disintegrator cannon.

"Don't want to take it in with you?"

She looked toward me and I nodded at the corner. She turned a little farther and the ridges were revealed again. This time, they were more neutral, a lighter shade of her bronze skin.

She ignored my question and turned back for the airlock. I walked over and grabbed the weapon, not having any intention of leaving it in plain sight. I turned and made sure she wasn't watching, then reached under my cot for a secret compartment where I hid the weapon.

Though I didn't particularly want to do so, I felt I should at least offer to help. "So, are you going to be okay? Do you need to be taken anywhere?"

I even surprised myself with how sincere I sounded.

"I'll be fine," she said, still without looking.

I was fed up with her attitude. "Most people would be glad to have their life saved."

"I'm glad you came around when you did, don't get me wrong." She drew a breath and gave me a stern look. "But you've gotten into something you can't possibly comprehend."

The mystery of her statement stoked my curiosity while I removed my blaster from its holster and laid it on my cot. "Try me."

At that moment, the pressurization routine ended and the hatch opened. Rione climbed into the airlock tube, then turned to me. "Sorry, fly boy, you'll find out eventually. Just be careful, somebody might not come along when you need saving."

Then she disappeared through the airlock. I was left with more questions, no answers, and now, what seemed to be a threat of things to come.

Chapter Three

By the time I climbed out the other end of the airlock tube, Rione was nowhere to be seen. It didn't break my heart being rid of her, as the short amount of time we'd spent together had already been too much as it was. I looked around and saw the computer terminal Jeanie had mentioned, embedded in the wall beside the hatch just as I'd been told. A red pad was positioned on the floor just this side of the terminal. I stepped over and looked at the small screen with no idea what I was doing.

"Mister West?"

I turned and saw a pale-skinned man in a flowing white robe. Out of instinct, my hand grabbed at the inside of my jacket, but came up empty, having forgot that I'd dropped my blaster off on my cot. I tended to leave my Mark II on the ship when I docked at unfamiliar stations or landed in a space port I had never been to before. Local authorities sometimes frowned, and sometimes jailed, upon weapons other than their own. And in this case, it just saved someone's life.

"Do I know you?"

"We have never met before this moment."

I stared down into his light blue eyes as the lights glinted off the blonde stubble atop his head. One thing was at the forefront of my mind. This may have been the mysterious buyer. "How do you know my name?"

"The station's crew obtained it through your galactic registration code, Mister West."

It was too bad he wasn't the buyer. I'd hoped for a hasty exit. "Why?"

"Our records indicate you have never before visited us. I am here to welcome you to our humble station, offer a tour, and answer any questions you may have."

His demeanor didn't seem to be a cover. Still, I had been sent this 'help' without asking, which set off warning alarms in my head. "Why the friendly treatment?"

His blue eyes did not waver. "Our people have always been introverts, since the beginning of our existence. When we finally expanded our presence beyond our planetary boundaries, it was decided to take after our galactic neighbors, the Rulusians."

My mind returned to the freighter, with the horrid images and smells of blaster-scorched carcasses. Fortunately, the Torian drew my attention back to the present. "We desire to keep relations with other species in good standing, so are friendly to all creatures who make their way to our station. We want to use our space presence as a means of diplomacy."

I shrugged. "Whatever works."

"It wasn't always that way. Until recent memory, our people were very xenophobic."

I tucked that tidbit away in the dark recesses of my mind and nodded. "So, what's your name?"

"Ecadin."

"Nice to meet you."

"Likewise. Now, Mister West, do you have any more questions, or would you like to take a tour of the station?"

"Actually, I do need some information." He smiled at the prospect. "I was told I'd need to pick up a cargo storage pass after I left the ship."

"Cargo storage passes are a means of identifying the owner of a cargo bay, and thus, only allow the owner access to the contents." I stepped aside as Ecadin moved in closer, and he pushed a number of buttons on the console beneath the screen.

He turned to me with one pale eyebrow raised. "Blue organic crystals? Is this correct?"

I nodded, but took his intrusion as extremely rude. Even though he probably hadn't meant any harm, the examination of my cargo had been insulting. If Torians planned their space presence as a means of diplomacy, they had a long way to go.

I only hoped all of their visitors were treated the way I was led to believe. I still had illegal cargo on my ship and needed to hurry this process along. It was possible they were on to me.

"To obtain a cargo storage pass, your identity must be scanned. Please step on the red pad." He motioned me over.

I followed his instructions and he entered a few more keystrokes into the console. At once, broad beams of red light flickered from above the screen, and scanned me from head to toe. Before I could even wonder what just happened, the beams disappeared. A small slot opened below the console and a tiny circular chip emerged. The Torian pulled it from the machine and placed it in the palm of my hand.

"That, Mister West, is your cargo storage pass."

"And if I want to sell this cargo?"

"There are numerous access terminals around the station, all with a red pad in front of them. The screen will guide you through the process." He smiled. "Would you like a tour of the station now?"

"Maybe another time, I'm in a rush." I paused a moment. "I do have one last question. I saw a hub in the center of your station, what's the quickest way to get there?"

He pointed at a small hallway to our left. “That corridor will take you directly to our hub, what we call the commons area.”

“Thanks, Ecadin.”

He gave a courteous nod, then walked off down the hallway in the opposite direction. A pair of Torians walked past with small energy weapons attached to their belts. I gave those security officers a wide berth and allowed them to pass the corridor, then started toward the hub.

• • •

As I walked into the commons area, I was immediately greeted with joyous laughter and murmurs of pleasant conversation. It was definitely a welcome change. Though Jeanie kept me company during longer trips, there was something to be said about contact with living beings.

A voice caught my attention. “Hey, you!”

I looked to my right, where a large figure in dark clothes sat against the wall.

“I’m sure a guy like you has a lady friend or two.”

I didn’t, but he kept up the pitch. “Wouldn’t you like to buy them some gifts?” He pulled out a metal case and flipped it open. A number of pieces of jewelry were displayed inside.

“Sorry, not interested.” I turned and walked off.

“You can get them real cheap,” he begged, but the crowd drowned out any further attempts to separate me from my money.

I looked around at various creatures as they made their way around the multitude of shops. There were some species I recognized and others I didn’t. Shop owners peddled their goods from doorways while enticing smells wafted over me. I had eaten at my last stop and with my body’s metabolism rate, wouldn’t need to for a while longer.

A Wasirian scurried past my feet, and nearly tripped me. He raised ten of his long green tentacles at me, insulted me with a phrase I wasn't familiar with and hurried off. I watched as his enormous bulbed head bobbed back and forth while he weaved in and out of the crowd. I just shook my head and walked toward the center of the room.

An announcement came over the speakers. "Transport service to Iyoria now departing from landing pad four."

I'd been there once, and never again. Gambling wasn't all that exciting, and there was nothing else to do there. Drinking reigned as my only true vice.

I looked around the room for anyone who may have been searching for me. I hadn't even been given a description of the buyer when I'd picked up the crystals, putting me at a significant disadvantage. Everyone I saw was occupied with their dining and shopping and paid me no attention. With some time to kill, I did the first thing that came to mind. My eyes caught sight of a sign over an entrance which spelled out 'Stardust' in bright yellow tubes, with advertisement signs plastered all over the establishment's windows, so I walked toward the place.

It was like no bar I'd ever seen. When people had every intention of becoming intoxicated in public, it tended to encourage rowdiness and roughhousing, at least in my experience. Stardust, on the other hand, was filled to the brim with peace and friendly voices. Two figures stood a head taller than myself, one on either side of the doorway. Brown cloaks covered their bodies and hoods shielded their faces from view. I guessed they were guards or bouncers, but I didn't plan to ask. I felt their eyes on me as I steered a path through numerous tables and sauntered up to an empty barstool along the right wall.

Immediately after I sat down, the barkeep came over. He seemed to be an older version of the Torian who had helped me before, with the same pale skin, blondish stubble, and light blue eyes. If he knew anything about me, though, he didn't let on.

"What can I get you?" His spirits were high, a trait I had never grown to like in anyone, especially bartenders.

"Anything good." I placed my elbow on the bar, and ran a hand down my face, then stifled a yawn.

The Torian reached down and pulled out a decanter filled with a pale red liquid, then a small glass. He filled the glass almost full, a sure sign of a decent barkeep, and slid it in front of me.

"Two credits."

I reached inside my jacket and put three on the counter. With the thought of riches in my immediate future, I felt generous. "Keep the change."

With the drink, however, he continued the conversation, "So, what brings you around these parts?"

Pity, I just started to like him.

"Just delivering some merchandise." I raised the glass to my lips and felt the smooth drink pass over my tongue.

I sat the half-empty glass back on the countertop. The barkeep mumbled, "Deliveries can be dangerous, especially around here."

"Only if the merchandise is illegal."

"We normally don't get those types of deliveries around here."

I took a smaller sip. "That's too bad. I know a lot of good people in the business."

He smirked and cleaned out a nearby glass. "I don't doubt it. You've probably done it yourself a time or two."

Had he not been right, I would have been offended. "Maybe. Maybe not."

I finished off the glass. He pulled the decanter back out, but I waved him off. There wasn't a point in getting too comfortable.

He placed the container down and wiped my glass with his wet cloth. "Don't get me wrong, friend. Everyone's welcome at my bar. Just keep an eye on your back. Toris isn't a safe place for outsiders and you can never be too sure who to trust."

"Why's that?"

He was reluctant, but went into a storytelling mode, as all good barkeeps do. "Torians have always been very xenophobic. For the longest time, our species did nothing but reside under the planet's surface."

"Sounds like a terrible way to live."

He set the glass on the counter and picked up another. "The surface of the planet has always been too cold and harsh for habitation, so most Torians never ventured out, save those in the military. As a result, most of us had no contact with species from other planets."

"But somehow that changed?"

"About seven revolutions ago, the subterranean thermal generator plants which supplied power for most of our cities were destroyed in a cave collapse. Those plants had been built hundreds of revolutions ago and no one knew how to fix them. We had no choice but to turn to other worlds for sources of power. Over time, we also learned new ways to design space ships and structures. This station, in fact, was a result of those efforts."

"So what does all of this have to do with Toris being unsafe for outsiders?"

"Let's just say not all Torians agree with a continued space presence." His eyebrow rose as he looked past me.

A hand grasped my shoulder from behind and I turned. A tall figure cloaked in brown cloth stood before me. At first, I figured it was one of the guards from the entrance, but a quick glance showed them both still standing at the doorway.

A deep and raspy voice spilled out from under the hood, "Aston West?"

I nodded.

"We have business to discuss."

Chapter Four

Not a word was said as we walked toward the far back corner of the establishment. The mysterious man picked a secluded table in the darkened recess and sat with the bar at his back. I'd learned long ago to always keep an eye on the entrance, so sat across from him. One of his cloak's arms was placed inside the other. My subtle attempts to peek under his hood failed.

"I assume you have brought the merchandise."

I pulled out the cargo storage pass and placed it on the table, anxious to get this job over and done with. "Ready and waiting."

"We shall get around to ownership transfer later. We have another job for you."

Money had been the reason I accepted a transport job in the first place. Another job this soon after the last would make life a little easier, financially. "I'm interested."

"I assume your ship is capable of passenger transport."

I crinkled my forehead. "It's a small transport, not a cruise liner. How many passengers are we talking?"

"Only one."

"Passengers require more attention than cargo. I'd like to know it's worth my while."

"Do not worry, we will make sure you are well compensated."

"Who's the passenger?"

He responded without hesitation, "We are sending our first representative to another world, and would like you to transport her."

"An ambassador?"

"Exactly. To maintain our space presence, we must learn about other cultures and teach our own to other species. To accomplish this, we will need representatives, ambassadors as you call them."

I thought back to my conversation with the barkeep. "I've heard not all Torians agree with this space presence."

A pause, before he continued, "It is unfortunate you have been told such things, Mister West, because they are simply unfounded lies."

"Then why enlist my services to transport her? Surely you have your own ships."

There was a brief moment of silence. "Our ships are not capable of speeds above the hyperspace threshold."

Something didn't sit right and what little trust I started with diminished to nothing.

"Now, would you be interested in our proposition?"

I couldn't outright decline the job, no matter my suspicions. Still, there were plenty of ways to sabotage the situation. "Transporting passengers won't come cheap."

"Finances are of no consequence. We are willing to pay any price necessary to ensure our space presence moves forward unhindered."

"Then you would pay triple the price of transporting these crystals?" I held up the pass.

He paused longer, then nodded once. "That would be acceptable. We shall pay you upon safe passage."

So much for sabotage.

I regained my composure. "So, when will I be picking up this ambassador?" I envisioned a long, boring trip with a monotone egotist. Hopefully, I could avoid a slow trip to insanity by drinking myself to oblivion.

"Talani will board this station in approximately two rotations, long enough for you to have a look around. She will meet you at your ship."

All thought of a hasty exit had just left my mind. "You've got yourself a deal."

He stood and I followed suit. "Now, we should take care of our immediate business," he told me.

I attempted small talk as the two of us started for a nearby terminal. "So, you must really like these crystals, to order an entire cargo container."

"Blue organic crystals were found in my tests to have the greatest strength, while still maintaining outstanding effects on power output. They were the best choice."

The pride on his tongue didn't escape my attention as I fished for information, "You've known my name this entire time. What's yours?"

"Larin Scath, Director of Defense." Then he second-guessed himself as we stepped up to the terminal. "That is of no consequence. Proceed with the transaction."

The two of us went through ownership transfer in a process as simple as I'd been led to believe. Within moments, the transfer was complete, and I had more credits in my accounts than there had been for as long as I could remember. I couldn't help thinking of the near future, when I'd get three times as much for transporting this ambassador Talani. The mere thought put a huge smile on my face.

Larin didn't even thank me as he scampered toward the front door. The two guards at the front doorway turned and escorted him on either side as he passed. I gazed at the barkeep and decided to return for another drink.

His eyebrows rose as I took another seat. "Strange company you keep, friend."

"As long as they pay me, and pay me well, that's all I worry about."

"Just heed my warning. You can never be too sure who to trust."

I pursed my lips a moment. "You have any Vladirian liquor?"

"A couple of bottles. New shipment's expected to come in after a few rotations."

"I'll take them both."

"You must really love Vladirian liquor." He chuckled.

I smiled. No one really understood my attachment to alcohol.

He walked over, reached under the counter and pulled out two bottles of the yellow murky liquid I love the most. "That'll be fifty credits."

I reached in my jacket and had to dig deep to meet the bill and give him a healthy tip. I placed the credits on the counter as he packaged the goods up in a small cushioned box. I wasn't sure what point it served, but let him go through the motions anyway.

"Enjoy, and come back again."

"Is there anywhere around here I could access my galactic accounts?"

"Access terminal is just across the commons area, next to the security office."

"Thanks." I picked up the box and walked out the door.

Everyone was still in a good mood out in the commons area as I regained my bearings. The terminal was tucked into a small alcove along the far wall and had I not been told where to look, I would have missed it. The commons area was lined around its circumference with dark grey panels, and depended on the individual shops to liven up the atmosphere. The crowd seemed to be lighter than when I'd first entered the Stardust, which suited me just fine, as I was able to avoid any more hucksters or accidental collisions on the way.

I stepped into the alcove and placed my thumb on the terminal screen. Within moments, my account information was available and I pulled a few hundred credits out of my now-healthy accounts.

I had plenty of time before meeting the ambassador, but wanted to get back on my ship. The barkeep's warning was gnawing at me, and I didn't want to stick around in a place where I might not be wanted.

I felt pretty good as I reached the second docking ring and turned the corner toward my ship. Two Torian guards, the same ones I'd seen walking past the port earlier, if I wasn't mistaken, stood just outside my airlock. A sense of fear permeated my brain as I thought of the three bays of illegal weapons in my hold. The guards' pale skin was bright under the ceiling illumination. Their light blue eyes stared me down and their mouths wore deep frowns. This wasn't going to turn out well.

The one on my left addressed me, "Aston West?"

I acted nonchalant. "Yes?"

Both of them raised their energy weapons. "You need to come with us, please."

At least he was polite. I attempted to stall the inevitable. "You want to tell me what you're doing?"

"Come with us peacefully and everything can be cleared up soon enough."

I was half-tempted to fight my way off the station, but logic prevailed at the moment I needed it most. I handed my box to the other guard, then turned and placed my hands behind my back. Electro-magnetic restraints tugged at my wrists as they marched me back down the vacant corridor.

• • •

The cell I was placed in was elegant as far as confinement went. In my youth, after leaving my home planet of Gryphon, I'd been placed in some of the worst in the galaxy. One which stood out from the rest was the prison planet Lycus IV. The species of the system, the Gohr, placed all manner of so-called violent criminals there to fend for themselves. I had spit in the face of a Gohr customs official, and been left to rot with rapists and murderers, among others.

Fortunately, I met up with two other prisoners I could trust, a pair of twin brothers, and we pulled off the first and only escape from Lycus IV. I hadn't seen Lars and Elijah Cassus since, but both would be ingrained in my memory forever.

I sat on a small cot and glanced out the transparent energy shield, where one of the guards from the docking port stood next to the entryway.

"I thought we were going to get everything cleared up. What happened?"

He ignored my comment and stared past me.

Beyond him, outside of my sight line, was the main booking area. I assumed that somewhere along the line, I'd get hauled before the local magistrate. Maybe then I'd find out what the official charges were, even if I had a fairly good idea.

I thought back to Lycus IV, where the trial had been a mockery, as everyone involved already set their minds toward your sentence before a verdict was even rendered. Between my arrest and being shoved on a transport for the prison planet, I don't think half a rotation passed.

"Can you at least give me a bottle of my liquor?" The box rested on the corner of a nearby desk. It relieved me to know they hadn't just disposed of it. I didn't know whether to take that as a good sign or not.

"Settle yourself down. Princess Wren will be here shortly."

Wonderful, I thought, I was in so much trouble, royalty was paying me a visit. And as if his comment was a summons, a youthful, attractive woman rushed into the room. Her flowing white robe accented her feminine features, while her light blond hair framed a blemish-free face. Her blue eyes were vibrant as she stared me down. This had to be the Princess.

Rione had a smug look on her face as she entered the room behind the Princess. Youthful and attractive were two things I could not, rather would not, say about my former travel companion. I was certain it didn't bode well as both of them came to a standstill just outside the field and the guard walked out of the room.

Rione's pale companion started off in a condescending tone. "I am Lucian Wren, Fourth Order of the House of Toris."

Even though it wouldn't help my cause any, I needed to vent my frustration, so stood and stormed up to the energy field. "Am I ever going to be charged with a crime, or do you just randomly lock people up?"

"Silence! The daughter of the King of Toris will not be spoken to in such a manner!" Her red-hot stare and angry tone would have forced a stake through a lesser man's heart. I wouldn't be intimidated by the likes of her, because I'd been through far worse.

I turned my attention back to Rione, who stood with her arms crossed. The princess continued, "You are charged with harboring illegal weapons."

I knew better than to believe Jeanie had failed to conceal my cargo from these people. "You have any evidence to back this up?"

"We have a witness who has testified to your criminal activities. This is all we require."

I kept my eyes on Rione. "And how do we know the witness isn't falsifying her testimony? Where I come from, witness testimony isn't allowed as accusatory evidence."

"I have personally vouched for the integrity of the witness."

I turned my attention to the Princess. "Funny how comfortable you are with the witness, considering you destroyed her freighter. Maybe you're trying to hide the fact she was harboring those weapons in the first place."

"Silence! I will not be insulted by someone as insignificant as you."

"The truth must hurt." I walked over and sat back down on the cot.

"You will be held for your hearing, at which time your fate will be determined. If you voluntarily hand over the contraband, perhaps the courts will have mercy on your miserable life and spare you a death sentence."

"Threats don't work on me, Princess." I laid down and stared at the ceiling.

"Consider it a promise." Her footsteps echoed on the tile floor as she left the room.

Unfortunately, she was the only one. Rione's voice carried into the cell, "Looks like you should have left when you had the chance."

I didn't bother looking. "Nice little setup you have, being cozy with the local leadership."

"Simple truth, fly boy. Those are my weapons, I want them back. And I'll get them, one way or another." She was so confident, I wanted to deck her.

"So, if harboring illegal weapons carries a death sentence, how do you get away with it? Pay them off?"

She growled under her breath. "I don't bribe people." She paused a moment, then returned to her earlier, confident tone. "I'm not the criminal here."

"Could have fooled me."

"The princess and I just happen to be close. She knows who I'm delivering the weapons to, and wants to help."

"Nice." I closed my eyes and tried to come up with a plan. I had no intention of dying here, nor of handing over my cargo.

"Why don't you just return what's mine, and save your own life this time?"

I rubbed my face. "I should have just dropped you off and left. The money would have been about the same, even with triple wages for transporting an Ambassador."

"What's this?"

I turned and glared. "What, you want to steal my next job?"

"A little bit of cosmic justice, for stealing my weapons in the first place."

"They would have been destroyed anyway. Of course, all my problems would be solved if I would have left your ship derelict."

She frowned at the implication. "So, are you going to tell me about this new job?"

"Might as well, it doesn't look like I'll be able to take it now." I stared at the ceiling panels. "I was supposed to transport a Torian ambassador."

"A Torian ambassador? Where were you supposed to take this ambassador?"

"I wasn't told." The promise of vast sums of money had eliminated my need for too many details.

"Who contacted you?"

"You sure have a lot of questions. Maybe you are going to steal it."

"Just curious."

"Some guy in a hood. I never saw his face. He said his name was Larin Scath." After she heard his name, her eyes grew wide and she bolted for the exit.

I jumped from the cot and stormed up to the energy field once again. "I can't believe this is how you're going to pay me back for saving your life."

She looked back toward me with a furrowed brow. "I'll see what I can do." Then, she raced out of the room, and the guard returned to the room and stood at the side of the doorway. I sulked over to the cot and plopped down once more.

I needed to get out of here. The trick was going to be in doing so without getting myself caught. Not that you could get in much more trouble than a death sentence, of course. I could have spared my life by giving up the cargo, but this was a matter of principle now.

I turned to the guard. "You're going to sit there and watch me every moment, aren't you?"

His stoic face told me what his voice didn't.

"Well, would you at least get me something to eat? I'm starving."

He folded his arms across his chest.

"Come on. Surely you feed your prisoners."

"I'll be right back," he mumbled.

As he stepped out of the room, I held up my arm and whispered into my transmitter, "Jeanie, can you hear me?"

"Aston, are you okay?"

"I've been better."

"According to the station's records, you've been incarcerated on weapons charges."

Jeanie had a tendency to be a bit nosy. I heaved a sigh. "Yes. Our guest informed them about our cargo."

"There had to be some explanation. I know they haven't defeated my efforts at concealing our cargo."

"I'm in a bit of a hurry here, Jeanie."

"I apologize."

"I'm in a holding cell."

"The station only contains one security area. What cell number are you in?"

I shifted myself on the cot to get a better look at the nameplates on the other doorways. "Looks like number three. Drop the energy field and keep it secret if you can."

"It doesn't appear they have very tight safeguards in place. It should only take a moment."

I jumped to my feet. "I'll be there in a little bit. You might want to prepare us for a departure whether the station lets us or not."

"Understood."

I walked up to the field and tried to get a better look past the doorway, just as the energy beams flickered and shut off.

I smiled. "Thanks, Jeanie. See you soon."

I grabbed my case of Vladirian liquor, scurried over to the doorway and eased my head out to look. Two guards sat at their desks with their backs to me, typing information into terminals. The guard who'd kept watch over me was nowhere to be seen, which suited me fine. I tiptoed out into the booking area, walked around the small counter, then bent down below the countertop just in case one of the two happened to turn around.

"Hey!"

I looked up and saw my guard with a tray of food, standing just inside the front door.

"Prisoner escaped!" He yelled to the others.

I rushed forward, nailing him in the midsection with my shoulder. He stumbled to the floor and I jumped over him on my way out.

As I ran into the commons area, I stopped and gathered my bearings. A few curious onlookers gave me odd glances, while others gave me a wide berth. I found the corridor I needed and sprinted for it. Voices yelled out behind me, but I paid them no heed as I rushed for my ship.

I raised my arm as I neared the second docking ring. "Jeanie, are you ready?"

"Affirmative."

A guard I didn't recognize stepped out from around the corner with his energy weapon drawn. I didn't have enough time to stop myself as a green blast struck me square in the chest. I stumbled and fell face-first to the floor, then slid to a stop against his feet. The box of liquor hit the floor beside me and thankfully stayed intact.

"Aston West, you're under arrest for attempted escape."

It was always a strange experience getting shot. My chest felt like it was going to explode from the inside, while I lost feeling in my extremities. Obviously, his weapon was set on a much higher setting than mine normally was. Then, my world slowly faded to black.

Chapter Five

Light slowly filtered through my eyelids and murmuring voices fell on my ears. I blinked and cleared my vision, while my body ached with disapproval of my escape attempt.

Rione's familiar voice came in loud and clear, "It looks like he's waking up."

I turned and looked in the direction of the voice. Princess Wren stood on the other side of the energy field with her arms folded across her chest. Rione stood at her side. The two of them were alone with my case of liquor back in its original location.

"An escape attempt has done nothing to help your cause, Mister West."

Rione smirked. "Some might even call it a stupid move."

I massaged my stiff neck. "I had nothing to lose."

"It has come to my attention you have been enlisted to transport our first ambassador to a new world."

I should have known better than to trust Rione with information. "And?"

She continued sternly, "Against my better judgment, I have decided to spare your miserable life and allow you to complete that mission."

Something wasn't right. People didn't just release you from a death sentence, especially after you attempted an escape. I had no intention, though, of denying her the chance to make a really bizarre decision.

"You are to be released immediately."

"It's about time." I rolled my legs off the cot, stood and limped toward the energy field, more than ready to leave.

Of course, there was always a catch. "You will, however, take Rione along with the ambassador. Also, you will turn over your contraband."

She could have pulled my heart out of my chest and caused me less pain. I pointed at Rione for added emphasis. "If you think I'm taking that backstabbing witch anywhere with me, you're sadly mistaken."

The princess was as stubborn as I was. "Either you accept our terms or you face the original punishment for your crimes."

I sulked and mulled over my options. I didn't have many, so I took my time.

She wasn't a patient one. "We await your decision."

My attitude kicked up a notch as I demanded, "I'll turn in the weapons, but keep her away from me."

"Not acceptable. It is imperative Rione stays with the ambassador."

She'd tipped her hand, so I kept up my bargaining, "Then if I have to take her along, let me keep my weapons."

"My weapons!" Rione argued.

I motioned toward her with both hands for the Princess' benefit. Unfortunately, the troublemaker wasn't tossed in a cell as I'd hoped.

"Silence!" Princess Wren's pale skin developed a reddish tinge. "You are not in a position to bargain."

I frowned as Rione leaned over and whispered in her ear. Wren's anger lifted and an evil smile covered her face. "So be it. We shall allow you to keep your contraband, in exchange for Rione's safe passage."

I had a bad feeling about their private conference, but a small victory was still a victory.

She clapped her hands twice, and two guards returned to the room. The first had been the one I'd attacked during my escape attempt and the other had been the one who attacked me.

"Escort him back to his ship."

She cut me off before I had a chance to protest. "Unless he would rather spend the time in his cell, which can still be arranged."

I kept silent. One of the guards stepped forward and shut down the energy field.

"To prevent any more escape attempts, restrain him until they're on his ship."

I scowled and complained, "That won't be necessary."

"I'm afraid it will be. Again, unless you prefer staying where you are."

I grumbled under my breath, "Fine."

The other guard walked behind me and placed my wrists back into a set of restraints.

"Someone at least grab my case of liquor."

Rione smirked, picked up the case, and led the way as we made our way out into the commons area. I wondered if sitting in the cell until I was ready to leave wouldn't have been the better choice. At least it would have been less embarrassing than being led around by the local authorities, with all the sidelong murmurs and looks of disdain.

The trip back into the corridor was quick, and we arrived back at the docking port without incident. The first guard motioned to Rione. "You first."

She walked toward the airlock, while I looked at the guard with disbelief. "Excuse me. I should be able to at least board my own ship first."

The guard behind me chuckled. "Don't need you trying anything."

The other told Rione, "We'll be right down the hall at the next guard station if you need any assistance. Don't hesitate to contact us."

I rolled my eyes as she disappeared into the tube. The guard behind me released the restraints and I rubbed my wrists before I followed her.

Climbing out into my living quarters moments later, Jeanie's voice greeted me, frantic, "Aston, are you okay?"

I exhaled a calming breath. "Yes, Jeanie."

"I've been worried, as you never arrived following your escape."

Rione laughed as she set the case of liquor down on my cot. "Failed escape."

"I have no intention of discussing it." My face burned red.

She smirked. "I know I wouldn't."

I glared at her. "I wouldn't have had to mess with an escape if you hadn't ratted me out."

Rione pointed at me. "Listen, you stole my property…"

"And saved your life, seems a fair trade to me. Though I'm debating that as I speak."

"Obviously, you don't have a bit of intelligence or you would have left after dropping me off. Is it my fault you're stupid?"

I'd had enough of her insults. "Just stay away from me, and when I drop the ambassador off, I'll finally be rid of you."

"Suits me fine."

I turned and stormed onto the bridge, then plopped into my Captain's chair. I reached down and grabbed my bottle from the side pocket. "Is an ambassador Talani on the station?"

I took a drink and waited a few moments as Jeanie searched the station's computer. "It does not appear any ambassadors, nor anyone by the name of Talani, have arrived at the station."

"Let me know when she does. We'll leave shortly after."

"Shall I lay in a course?"

"I'll give you the destination as soon as it's given to me."

"Acknowledged."

I sat back in my chair, closed my eyes, and turned my mind to more pleasant thoughts. This one last job was all I had to get through. Then I'd be rid of both Rione and the ambassador, and have enough credits to last me a good long while. The mere thought of some financial security put a smile on my face as I dozed off.

• • •

The next thing I knew, Jeanie's voice brought me back to reality as she told me, "Aston, someone has requested permission to board."

My heart pounded against my chest with the sudden interruption.

"Who is it?"

"She claims to be the ambassador."

"And you don't believe her, I take it?"

"I've monitored the station records since we last spoke. There has been no change. No ambassador has boarded this station, nor anyone named Talani."

At least that explained the lack of advance warning.

"How long have I been out?" I rubbed my face.

"Approximately half a rotation."

I stood and started toward the back. "Certainly doesn't feel like it."

Rione sat at my circular table, which rested in the far corner opposite my cot. Her stare was blank and fixed on the table's center. She blinked in rapid succession and looked over at me.

Cheerful as ever, she spoke, "What are you doing back out here?"

I tried to be civilized. Our trip would go a lot smoother without the two of us at each other's throats. Besides, I'd be rid of her soon enough and I definitely looked forward to that moment. "Good morning to you, too."

Her bitter tone told me she was keeping the gloves off. "Actually, it's mid-afternoon."

I suffocated the coming argument. "The ambassador is here. We'll depart shortly."

She crossed her arms and frowned, while I shook my head and crawled through the airlock tube. I climbed out the other side a short while later, where another figure waited under the full cover of a cloak and hood.

I had no idea how to greet her. My time with the Torian princess hadn't been a learning experience, for sure.

"Ambassador Talani?"

Her voice was cold and the female match to Larin Scath's. "Mister West."

"I apologize for the delay. We didn't catch your name on any incoming passenger logs." I raised an eyebrow and attempted to get a subtle glimpse under the hood, failing miserably.

"I have been told you are aware of the feelings some hold toward our efforts at space diplomacy."

I gave a slight nod. "So I've been told."

"As a result, I am travelling under an assumed name."

Rather odd, I thought, but it made sense in a way. "Whatever works."

"Are you prepared to depart?"

"Whenever you are." Deep in my gut, I knew Talani was going to be as much fun to be around as Larin Scath had been.

I stepped aside as she picked up two metallic cases and thrust them into the tube. I followed her in. Rione and the ambassador were already locked in a death stare by the time I planted my feet back on my ship.

The ambassador growled, "Who is this?"

"Another passenger." I stepped between the two of them on my way to the bridge.

"This is unacceptable."

"This is how it's going to be." I was irritated with this entire situation and was already sick of them both.

Rione retorted, "Hope I'm not scaring you."

"No one scares me, especially the likes of you."

"Ambassador, where am I supposed to be taking you?" I was here to do a job, and didn't plan to put myself in the middle of their petty squabble.

My demands took the fight out of her, as her voice calmed, "Rulusia."

The coincidence was not lost on me, nor on Rione who matched stares with me. She went on the attack with a biting question, "Taking a personal trip?"

"That is none of your concern."

She pointed at the ambassador's cases. "What do you have in those?"

"I am on official government business, you piece of common trash. If you must know, besides clothing for myself, I'm carrying a trade agreement for the Rulusians to sign."

I decided to let the two bicker amongst themselves while I grabbed my case of liquor and my holster. "We'll head out shortly."

The ambassador caught me before I could reach the doorway. "Do you have any other place I can rest? I have no intention of residing in the same room with garbage." She motioned toward Rione, as if I needed her to.

"Afraid there's not much more than what you see here. Cargo bay two is open, back there." I pointed toward the cargo hold. "It's not very comfortable and really isn't meant for occupancy."

I wasn't even sure if it had warmed up to a livable level.

"It will do much better than this." She picked up her cases and stormed off.

Rione got in the last word, "Don't accidentally eject yourself out into space. We wouldn't want that to happen." Fortunately for me, the ambassador ignored her.

"I don't like her," Rione muttered under her breath after Talani left.

"You don't have to like her. You just have to leave her be until we reach Rulusia."

"Let me rephrase." She placed her elbows on the table and interlaced her fingers. "I don't like her, and don't trust her either."

"I don't trust you, and you're coming along."

"Cute," she snarled

I continued to the cockpit and transferred the case's contents into a recessed storage cooler behind the co-pilot's seat. "You heard the ambassador, I assume. Lay in a course for Rulusia."

Jeanie's response was immediate. "The waypoints are already set."

I smirked. "Always a step ahead, aren't you?"

"Always."

I reached over to the aft half of the center console, and transmitted a message to the station. "This is Sierra-Tango-Four-Two-Four, requesting departure clearance."

"Clearance is granted, Four-Two-Four. Departure coordinates are being transferred to your navigation computer." I looked over at the sensor screen on the left wall, and saw them pop up. "From that point, you'll be cleared from station control. Have a nice trip, and hope to see you again."

I feigned politeness. "Thanks." After the treatment I'd received, I didn't plan on ever coming back.

Jeanie interrupted, "Depressurization is complete. We are ready to proceed."

"Take us out." We moved away while the flashing lights waved goodbye.

While we covered the distance to the departure coordinates, I strapped my holster in place under my jacket. "How are our passengers?"

"Rione is still in the living quarters. The ambassador is in cargo hold two."

"This is going to be a long trip."

"It should be much shorter than our last journey."

I knew she was right from a sheer time standpoint, and didn't press the issue as we both fell silent on the trip out.

"We've reached the coordinates."

"Hyperspeed."

The acceleration pushed me into my seat and I watched thin trails of white starlight race off the sides of the screen. I was glad to put Toris behind me forever.

Chapter Six

I'd been shot at, threatened, imprisoned, verbally abused, and nearly sentenced to death. This definitely wasn't my finest hour. I reached over and grabbed for my bottle. Before I even had a chance to open it, Rione stepped onto the bridge behind me. I unscrewed the cap and gulped down some of the sweet yellow liquid while she crossed her arms and stood there in silence.

"Accommodations not to your liking?"

"Just the company."

"Go sleep for a while. It'll make the trip pass quicker." I spoke from experience.

"I can't believe that you don't care what this woman is doing on your ship."

"As long as I'm getting paid, I really don't."

She took a seat in the other chair and faced me. "Toris doesn't have ambassadors, Aston."

"Again, not my problem." I shrugged and took another drink.

"Do you think it's just coincidence a fictitious ambassador is sent to Rulusia after my Rulusian freighter is caught smuggling weapons?"

I'd already thought about it and had more questions than answers. "I guess it depends on what those weapons were for, doesn't it?" She turned toward the front and I grunted, "Glad to see some things never change."

"I wish I could tell you, but that's not possible."

"I wish I could be concerned about Talani, but that's not possible either."

She looked back at me. "Are you going to search her belongings?"

"Just because you don't trust her doesn't give me the right to go through her stuff." I held no trust for the ambassador either, but I wouldn't give Rione the satisfaction.

"It's your ship."

"She's a paying passenger, unlike some people."

"You don't understand who she is."

"I'm open to you explaining it to me. Have you met her before?"

"I've met people like her and those she associates with."

"It's going to take a bit more than that, I'm afraid," I said with a chuckle, then drank.

She fidgeted a moment, before scowling. "Are you going to search her bags or am I going to have to do it myself?"

"Afraid you're on your own."

She stood and stormed out of the cockpit. She was going to pick a fight, and the truth was, I didn't care.

Jeanie piped up, "Do you plan to stop them from injuring each other?"

I'd had my fill of both of them, but knew I wouldn't get paid if Talani wasn't delivered alive. I leaned back and sighed. "I'll give them a little bit to get it out of their system, and then head back to break it up."

The ensuing silence was golden, but like all good things, short-lived. "Rione has been locked into cargo bay three."

I closed my eyes and massaged my temples. "Ambassador Talani…"

"Yes. She was able to use the manual controls."

"Engage the override locks before she does something stupid like dump the bay." I was more worried about the illegal weapons still in that cargo bay.

"Done." She paused. "Shall I open the bay and release Rione?"

I was tempted to leave her there for the duration of the trip, but knew it was the right thing to do. "Let me settle the ambassador down first."

"Talani has reached the override and has returned to bay two."

I stood and walked back to the cargo hold. I looked down the empty corridor and shook my head. This would be the last time I ever transported passengers for anyone, paying or not.

I used the keypad next to bay two, and the hatch slid open. Talani sat on the floor at the center of the room, legs crossed underneath her. Her cases rested in front of her. At least the bay had warmed up since Jeanie had transferred the crystals to the station. "So, you locked my other passenger in a cargo bay?"

She was caught off-guard by my question, and stood before responding, "She was becoming annoying and rude, and demanded to search my belongings."

Without Rione present, I could be frank. "I can't say I blame her."

She tilted her head to one side while the door closed behind me. "Why would you say such a thing?"

"Personally, I don't tend to trust people I can't see face to face."

She reached up in silence and pulled her hood down. I was taken aback at her features, which put even Princess Wren to shame. Her pale skin reminded me of an expensive figurine with its smooth, sculpted lines. Her eyes were the brightest shade of blue I had ever seen, as she stared at me.

"Do you trust me now?"

"Trust is earned," I muttered under my breath.

I'd been around enough to know a pretty face could be a path to disaster. Still, I found it difficult to keep my focus off her appearance. I'd definitely been without companionship far too long.

"Fair enough," she told me.

"This entire squabble with the other passenger makes no sense to me."

She had an answer for everything. "She's harassed me since I came aboard."

"You only have to put up with her until the trip is over."

"That will be too long to wait."

"I'd better go let her out." I looked back at the hatch.

"Wait!"

I turned at the sound of her voice and she walked closer. Her head came to the same height as mine and I stared into those bright blue eyes as she put her hands on my chest.

Warning bells went off in my head as she purred, "Wouldn't you like to leave her back there? We could be alone."

Half of me was tempted, but the other half was confused at the sudden burst of affection. It didn't make for a good feeling. "I'm afraid I still don't trust you."

"Why not?"

"You have too many secrets, like those two cases. I know you told us what's in them, but how can I be sure you're telling the truth?"

"Do you really want to see?"

"Yes."

She moved over with calm confidence toward the cases on the floor. I watched as she laid the first down and opened the lid. She reached inside and pulled out a small energy pistol.

I didn't have time to grab my Mark II from its holster, so backed up toward the wall. "Whoa, what's this?"

She went back to her cold, calculated tone. "The end of your life, Mister West."

"Why?"

"Because you know too much."

I begged to differ. "I obviously don't know enough."

"Your services are no longer required. You've given us what we need."

The hatch slid open and Rione jumped through, a disintegrator cannon in her hands.

"Drop it," she demanded.

Talani traded glances between us, then swung the pistol around at Rione, who fired the cannon. I flinched out of instinct as the blast struck the ambassador square in the chest, slamming her against the wall. The energy dissipated through her body and decomposed her flesh and internal organs amidst agonizing screams, until there was nothing but a pile of organic ash on the floor. I was glad I hadn't met the same fate on the freighter.

At least Rione lowered her weapon as she turned and yelled at me, "You idiot! Why didn't you come back and help me?"

"I was trying to."

"At least your computer was smart enough to let me out."

She walked over and knelt next to the remains. I, on the other hand, kept a respectable distance. The thought of being close to a disintegrated corpse didn't appeal to me and the smell of burnt flesh had already wafted over. She shoved her hand into the pile, pulled Talani's weapon out, and shook it off.

"An electro-discharge pistol set to maximum output. Looks like she was going to kill you off."

She looked over with pursed lips. "I guess this makes us even, fly boy."

"Thanks." I wasn't one to take the preservation of my life lightly, unlike some.

"What was she trying to kill you for?"

"I wish I knew." Normally, when someone wanted to take my life, I had a good idea why. "She mentioned something about me knowing too much, that my services were no longer required."

"What services did you provide?"

There was only one thing which tied me to the ambassador. "I'll share what I know if you do the same."

She was reluctant, but nodded.

"I was hired to transport a container of blue organic crystals to a buyer on the orbital station in the Toris system. That was Larin Scath, the guy who set this up."

The guy who set me up to be killed. To top it off, I wouldn't get the credits I'd been promised. I should have asked for payment in advance.

"What were they going to be used for?"

"I don't know the particulars, I didn't bother to ask."

"Well, whatever they were for, it's obvious they don't want you around."

"Obviously."

"Let's check her things and see if we can figure out what else she was going to do. If they wanted you dead, they could have just destroyed your ship like they did mine. It seems like a lot of trouble to do the job personally."

I wouldn't let her stall forever. I wanted answers. "Fine, we search her things, then you tell me what I want to know."

Rione nodded and rummaged through the case Talani had pulled the weapon from. "Looks like these are just her clothes."

I stepped over and opened the other case, which was stacked full of papers. I picked up the top half and handed it over. "See what you can find. I'll look through the rest."

We sat down on the bay floor and sifted through the documents. I counted paperwork for three separate identities. Whoever she was, she hadn't wanted anyone to track her.

Rione updated me, "All I'm finding here is a trade agreement. She definitely wanted to make sure everything looked okay on the surface."

Near the middle of my stack was a piece of paper that caught my attention. Times were listed, along with scribbling for each in a language I didn't recognize. One of the times was circled. I handed the sheet to Rione. "Seems to be a schedule. The only question is whose?"

"Looks like Torian writing." She paused a moment to scan the document, then went pale.

"What's wrong?"

She looked over at me and trembled. "She was going to assassinate the Rulusian President."

"What? Why?"

"I don't know. Hopefully we find more information."

I returned to my stack, where I found a one-way ticket on a passenger transport from Rulusia to the Yries system. I'd only heard stories and never visited, but it had always sounded like a place to avoid. Laws were nonexistent there and it was near impossible to get the government to extradite anyone. So, in essence, it was the perfect place to flee a crime and hole up for a while. I tossed the ticket to Rione.

She examined it while I offered up my own theory, "Looks like she wanted to make a clean getaway."

"But what sense would it make to do anything against the Rulusians? They're on good terms with the Torians."

"Maybe someone in the Torian government isn't too pleased a Rulusian freighter was carrying illegal weapons into their system."

She frowned. I decided now was the moment to get the promised information. "What happened on your ship? Who were those weapons for?"

"I still can't tell you."

I called out to Jeanie. "Drop us out of hyperspeed and come to a full stop."

The ship lurched as she obeyed my command.

Rione cursed under her breath. "What are you doing?"

"We're not going anywhere until you give me some answers."

She sighed, but knew I was serious. "We were on our way to Toris to deliver weapons from Rulusia. As soon as we came out of hyperspeed, we had a squadron of fighters and a troop transport right on top of us."

"Sounds like somebody let them know you were coming."

She nodded. "Anyway, the fighters were able to disable us, but I've had hull modifications which made my ship thicker than a standard freighter, so they couldn't finish the job."

That explained why the fighters hadn't been around when I showed up.

She continued, "After they boarded my ship, everything went south. The crew was getting massacred and my officers and I were holed up in the bridge. My first officer hid me inside the cargo hold when they tried to storm the bridge. Next thing I know, you showed up."

Fortunately she spared any recollection about trying to kill me.

"Then the cruisers returned to finish the job?"

She nodded.

"So who are the weapons for?"

"Torian freedom fighters."

"Freedom fighters?"

"Some Torians think differently than the government. To quell what they see as divergent thinking, they kill them."

I remembered the barkeep on the station. "Because they believe in interstellar contact?"

She seemed surprised. "You're not as stupid as you look, fly boy. Of course, it's just one of many points of contention. They have different opinions about leadership, class structure, and many other things. The end result is the same."

"Why don't they just leave?"

"It's their home, too. If they have to fight for their rights, then so be it."

I thought it was pretty stupid, but if they wanted to kill themselves for their beliefs, it was their call. "And where do you fit in with all of this?"

"I was in a similar situation on my home world, so I empathize with the rebels." She pulled her hair back to display her ridges. "I'm from a planet called Lazarus. Small minorities of us are born with these emotion ridges. People feared us because we looked different, so the government wanted to kill us. Unfortunately, there weren't enough of us to organize a rebellion, so we were forced to flee to escape death."

"And how are the Rulusians involved?"

"They want to maintain good relations with Toris, something that won't happen if the current leadership gets their way."

"So help change the leadership?"

"They gave me a ship, and I found a crew willing to help. The rest you know." Her eyes drooped.

"Well, you can fight your little civil war if you want, but I don't plan to stick around long enough to see if this one turns out any different than any other."

"Why don't you help out? We're going to need another ship to transport more weapons, and I wouldn't doubt you could get the job done."

Now she was trying to patronize me.

"Sorry, no dice. I'm a scavenger pirate. I gave the soldier life up a long time ago."

"Don't you care about these people dying for no reason? Where's your sense of justice?"

"It's falling right there behind my sense of wanting to live past tomorrow."

Her tone soured, "I'd bet you'd do it if there was enough money in it for you."

Pity, we'd just started to get along.

"No amount of money would be worth going through what those people will be."

"Then what do you plan to do?"

"Once I drop you off, I'll probably hang out on Rulusia for a while, visit an old friend. Then, I'm leaving. Of course, if you're planning to imprison me again, I'll skip the first part."

"I told the princess I would convince you to help us."

I figured they'd schemed against me. "Sorry to disappoint."

"Since we're heading to Rulusia, though, I can get a fresh shipment and a new ship. Trying to get you to turn over those weapons is a fight I'll never be able to win."

At least with the weapons, I'd be able to cover up the lost wages from this botched passenger transport job.

I looked at Talani's remains, then turned to Rione. "Let's head back to the living quarters."

She grabbed the cases and we stepped back out into the corridor. I turned to the keypad, pressed a few buttons and locked the bay.

"So, once we get to Rulusia, we'll let the investigators check out her remains. Maybe they'll glean some more insight into her motives."

"I don't plan on letting her remains make it to Rulusia."

"But we might be able to determine who she is."

I pressed a few more buttons on the keypad and the bay went through an emergency decompression cycle, which would blow Talani's ashes out into the vacuum of space.

"I see no need for the authorities on Rulusia to find a disintegrated corpse on my ship."

"Why do you always have to be so difficult?" She stormed off.

"Jeanie, resume course."

Chapter Seven

I was too wired to sleep through the remainder of the trip. It wasn't a common occurrence for someone to end up disintegrated on my ship. Jeanie finally announced our arrival, "Now entering the Rulusian system."

We dropped back into regular space and the viewscreen lit up with the bright images of a binary star. Most of the ones I'd ever seen, the stars would move one around the other. Here, however, the two stars remained fixed while Rulusia itself was caught in a double elliptical orbit, slicing a path between the two stars twice during its annual cycle.

"Set us up for a standard parking orbit, Jeanie."

"Acknowledged."

The ship turned to the left, and I caught a glimpse of the planet once the full brightness of two stars wasn't shining directly in front of me.

"At least we won't have to mess with seismic activity," I mused. The planet had a tendency to have significant earthquakes when travelling between the two mammoth stars. I'd had the misfortune of experiencing it firsthand the last time I'd visited Rulusia, during my youth.

I'd stayed with my good friend, Crillian Castril, during that trip, and was hoping to do the same this time. The planet grew larger, until I made out the outline of continents. Rione walked into the cockpit.

Before I could say anything, Jeanie interrupted, "I'm picking up two Rulusian AI-5s on an intercept course."

Catching up with the local military after dropping out of hyperspace was getting to be a regular occurrence I could do without.

I watched the two fighter-interceptors close the distance, then break formation and disappear off the sides of my viewscreen. I anticipated the worst, though I had done nothing wrong as far as the Rulusians knew.

They eased up on either side of me. "Sierra-Tango-Four-Two-Four, welcome to Rulusia."

"Thank you," I responded with uncertainty.

"We already have a landing pad approved for your arrival in the capital. The Minister of Interstellar Affairs is waiting."

I watched as the thin cylindrical vessels passed in front of me, their stubby wings useless in the vacuum of space. I didn't know what to make of the fact that they seemed to know I was coming, let alone that a Minister was waiting for me. I simply gave a weak, "Acknowledged."

Jeanie altered our course and speed to match the two escorts. Three exhaust nozzles on each ship cast a bright white glow, even though both were more than a safe distance away. We entered the upper atmosphere and a gigantic tropical forest appeared below us. Extra-large, dark green leaves in the treetops blocked the jungle floor from view.

One of my escorts spoke, "Coordinates are being transferred."

I looked over at the sensor screen and saw my destination pop up a moment later.

During my last visit, Crillian had told me stories about a number of beasts out in the wild. One I remembered was a four-legged furry beast, which dropped on its prey, then ripped entire limbs from its victims with giant claws and tore flesh apart with a multitude of fangs. Not a pleasant thought, whether it was truth or tall tale, and the stories alone had ensured I'd never gone beyond the walls of the capital city.

I looked over at my travelling companion with a new worry that popped into my mind. "It sounds like they're expecting an ambassador and we don't have one handy."

"Nothing to worry about."

"Easy for you to say."

As we leveled out and continued our journey, light glinted off the tallest buildings in the capital. Getting closer, the vast sea of buildings stretched in every direction. A convoy of freighters launched from an acceleration tunnel to my left.

Jeanie slowed us down a short while later. We began a gradual descent toward a landing pad, while our escorts hovered above. "The Minister is waiting."

"Thanks." I turned my attention toward the landing pad, confident of Jeanie's ability to make a perfect landing. The landing skids deployed amidst a shrill whine and the main landing thrusters fired. Moments later, we thudded to rest on the pad and I watched the fighter-interceptors break left toward parts unknown.

I turned back to Rione. "Well, looks like we'll see whether you're right."

"Worried?"

"With you around, always."

Jeanie powered down the engines, and the viewscreen shut down while the lights dimmed. Rione and I walked to the back where she grabbed the two cases.

"Think that's wise, considering we don't have the ambassador on-board?"

"I told you not to worry about it."

I shrugged and double-checked my holster. I had no intention of being without a weapon around her ever again. Plus, if memory served, Rulusian law allowed for concealed weapons to be carried for defense. "I'll keep worrying about it until I'm free and clear of you."

She smirked. "Trust me."

I smoothed out my jacket. "I trusted you last time, and see where it got me." She ignored me as the entry hatch opened to a set of airstairs.

Memories of Rulusia flooded back to my mind as soon as my feet touched the black landing pad. Sweat poured down my face and a salty bitterness coated my lips. Both stars hung low in the sky, but had already dispensed their full load of heat for the day.

"Where's the Minister?"

"He'll be here," she insisted, which only drove me to worry more.

Waves of heat floated along the pad and distorted my view of a small building in the corner. Rione started toward the structure and I followed. A side door on the building opened a few steps later and two Rulusians emerged in all-black dress uniforms with blast rifles slapped across their chests.

My instincts told me to make a break for it. I'd been down this road before, and not very long ago. I had no intention of going through a repeat of my visit to the Torian orbital station. Before I had time to act, the two stepped aside and another green figure walked out in a flowing, white robe. I stopped in my tracks and looked over at Rione, who had a smile on her face. The idea of her being in good graces with local government officials did nothing to ease my nerves.

Rione turned as I fell behind. "What are you doing?"

"If it's all the same, I'd prefer not to get thrown in another holding cell."

"You could try to run, but you'd probably get yourself shot instead." She smirked.

That was a sobering thought.

"Now stop being so paranoid."

"It's not paranoia when I know you're out to get me."

She blew off my comment and continued, "I already told you I planned to get a fresh shipment of weapons. With that in mind, what would I need to blackmail you for?"

"I still have a ship."

She rolled her eyes. "There are plenty of other ships available on Rulusia."

It was a moot point as the Minister reached the two of us. "Rione, it's good to see you again." He reached for her hand, leaned down and kissed it.

She gave a slight nod. "Minister."

He turned to me with dull gray eyes. "Pardon my manners. I am Ba'lor Bilhari, Minister of Interstellar Affairs." He extended his hand, jagged teeth forming a smile which could give small children nightmares.

"Aston West."

He returned his attention to my companion. "Rione, I am surprised to see you return so soon. I would have expected the delivery to take much longer."

"We ran into a snag."

"A snag?"

I wouldn't have considered the same chain of events so lightly, but kept silent.

"How much has the Princess told you?"

"Not much, I'm afraid. We couldn't access a secure channel."

"My freighter was ambushed as soon as we entered Torian space. Somebody let them know we were coming."

"Then it's as we suspected, and there's a leak."

"It appears so."

Sweat was a waterfall on my face. "If you two wouldn't mind, could we take this conversation inside?"

Rulusians had a tendency for exaggerated facial expressions and Ba'lor was no different. His eyes went wide as he realized I still stood there.

"Most definitely. I often forget how inhospitable our climate is to other species."

He turned to Rione and I followed his gaze. Her hair was damp and her red top clung tight to her curves, so I focused back on the Minister. The last thing I needed to do was find her attractive after everything she'd put me through.

Ba'lor led us toward the small building, while our armed escorts trailed behind. I walked a few steps behind Rione and the Minister while they continued their discussion.

"Now, my dear, tell me more about this ambush."

She gave a similar account to the one she'd given me. Then, she thumbed in my direction. "If not for Aston arriving when he did, I probably wouldn't be around to tell the tale."

He turned his head and nodded toward me. "It appears we owe you a debt of gratitude."

At least someone thought so.

"We also uncovered evidence of a more sinister plot."

"Oh?" His forehead bunched.

I took the lead on this one. "I was enlisted to transport a woman who claimed to be a Torian ambassador."

"Toris has ambassadors? Since when?"

"They don't." Rione grimaced as she held up the two cases. "These hold information which makes us think she planned to assassinate the Rulusian President."

We walked inside the building and out of the sweltering heat. Unlike their ships, Rulusians kept their building comfortable, at least when there was a likelihood outsiders would be present. At the far end of the cramped, air-conditioned waiting room, the lower half of the wall was gone, and in its place was a large, clear tube.

One of the guards pulled a small rectangular transmitter off his belt and spoke in a deep, monotone voice, "Send a political transport to sector thirty-seven, pad B."

Without warning, a huge cylinder raced into the room through the tube and came to an abrupt stop. I remembered this amazing piece of technology from my last visit to Rulusia, which seemed forever ago. It traveled not on wheels or rails, but magnets embedded both in the tube walls and the transport itself. On-board computers analyzed exactly the route to take and controlled speed, direction, and acceleration. All of this, and it still knew how to avoid colliding with the thousands of other transports in the system at any given moment.

One of the guards walked over to the vehicle and lifted the door. Inside, the interior was ornate, with plush bench seats at the front and back of the compartment, and thick carpet on the floor, all a deep red color. The walls on all four sides were off-white. There were no windows, so we would be at the total mercy of the computer. From memory, this wasn't the look and feel of your everyday transport.

"Please, have a seat." Ba'lor motioned toward the open door.

Rione and I sat at the back of the car, while the Minister and his guards entered and faced us. The last guard pressed a button on the side frame next to him and the door slowly closed while we buckled in. Even so, the compartment was lit up even brighter than it had been on the landing pad.

Rione adjusted the cases at her feet. "We need to let the President know about this."

Ba'lor nodded. "We should also have investigators look through those cases more thoroughly. Perhaps they can gain more information."

I interjected. "If it's all the same, I'd just like to be dropped off at a friend's…"

Rione looked at me in disbelief. "Don't you care about anyone besides yourself? This woman planned to assassinate an important official. She almost killed the two of us, and you couldn't care less."

"It's not a matter of caring." I paused for a deep sigh. "Nothing good has come from this situation, so the sooner I'm out, the better."

Rione frowned, then opened her mouth, but Ka'lor jumped in, "Mister West, we thank you for your assistance. And we would be more than happy to take you anywhere you want to go."

"I don't recall his address and wouldn't even know if he still lived there anyway. All I have is a name."

He gave me his jagged-toothed smile again. "That is all we need."

"Crillian Castril."

Ba'lor spoke to the computer. "Residence of Crillian Castril, please."

I was forced against the seat cushion as the transport rapidly accelerated. Even though I couldn't see where we were going, every twist, turn, rise and fall wreaked havoc on my insides.

Then, before I even realized it, the restraints strained against my chest and we came to a stop. One of the guards reached over and opened the door with a press of the button.

As I unbuckled, Ba'lor gave me another smile. "Again, Mister West, we thank you for your assistance. If ever you venture into this system again, please drop by."

I wasn't fond of politicians, so doubted I'd ever see him again. I just nodded and climbed out of the transport.

"Have a good life, fly boy," Rione called out.

I turned as the guard pressed the button once more. The door eased shut, before the transport rushed out of the room. I warmed up immediately, but at least it wasn't as unbearable as the conditions outside had been.

My boots clopped on the hard gray tile as I walked across the room toward an entry door. Like at the landing pad, this room had three walls and a transport tube along the fourth. I was completely alone and the emptiness was just plain eerie. There was also no reason for it, as the capital city was congested and living space was limited. At least it had been last time I was here. In my experience, gigantic cities never got smaller.

As I approached the door, a voice echoed in the emptiness. "Name, please."

I was taken aback, and it took a moment for me to answer. "Crillian Castril."

"Room three-thirteen. Thank you. Have a nice day."

I shook my head at the lack of security measures, then pulled the door open and walked inside.

I'd seen some horrid living conditions in my life, but this was one of the worst. The carpet was torn, in some places all the way down to the bare floor. Walls were partially covered, with some wallpaper peeling off, the rest ripped in wide swaths. Occasionally there would be a hole smashed through the side panels. I didn't even want to think about where the stains came from which graced the floors and walls and in some places, even the ceiling. As I walked along the corridor, I noticed about a third of the lights above functioned. And to top it off, a putrid odor lingered in the air and made me want to vomit.

I braved the conditions and continued down the hallway to a tee intersection. Tape barricades prevented entry to two open doorways in front of me. I leaned over the barrier and open shafts reached down into darkness. On a whim, I lifted up my sleeve and spoke, "Jeanie, are you out there?"

There was no response, which meant the transport had taken me out of range.

A sign hung on the wall between the two openings and pointed me to the left. With another look of disbelief at the scenery, I shook my head and started in that direction. A little farther down the hallway, on the right hand side, I found a door with the room number marked in heavy ink.

It had been a long time since we'd seen each other, and I hoped he recognized me. I wondered what I would say if he didn't, but took a deep breath and rapped my knuckles on the hardwood anyway.

Footsteps approached, creaking over floorboards inside. The door opened ever so slightly and a single black eye peeked out through the gap. He blinked fast a couple of times as his memory jogged into action. "Aston?"

Chapter Eight

I was so surprised he'd actually recognized me, let alone remembered my name, I forgot to respond. A moment later, I nodded and the door flew open. Before I was able to prepare myself, he rushed out and locked his arms around me. My ribs felt like they would crack under the pressure of his friendly embrace. He let loose his death grip and stepped back, allowing me to finally take a deep breath. A large smile was plastered to his dark green face, while the dim light glinted off his bald head.

"How have you been, friend?" He asked.

I smiled. "In trouble, of course."

He stepped aside and motioned toward the open door. "Where are my manners? Come inside."

I stepped into the apartment and Crillian shut the door as he followed me in.

I was glad to see his apartment was in better shape than the rest of the building. The living room we entered was neat and orderly, with a pair of couches nestled in the corner to our right. A short wall with a bar counter separated off the kitchen at the back of the room, while a hallway led off beyond. Crillian directed me to one of the couches.

He adjusted some papers on the table in front of us and leaned back, as the lamp in the corner highlighted the left side of his face. "How long has it been?"

"Quite a while."

Crillian shook his head. "It doesn't seem like it."

"No, it doesn't." I sighed. "Time just has a way of creeping up on you, I suppose."

The truth was, I never forced myself to take a detour and visit as I should have.

I continued, "So, what are you up to nowadays?"

"Same old thing, still freelance reporting for galactic news outlets."

"At least it's somewhat stable."

He contorted his forehead. "What do you do now? I know you told me you were getting out of the Defense Force, but that was a long time ago."

"Dad?" A female voice caught us both unaware. I turned and saw a young woman in the hallway arch.

"Hey, baby. Look who stopped by."

The room fell silent. Crillian looked over at me. "Aston, I don't know if you remember my daughter, Juniper."

She stared at me with dark blue eyes and a thin smile. Thin strands of white hair hung down to her waist, bleached by constant exposure to excessive star light. Despite my best efforts to ignore it, her body had matured in all the right places. Her pale green skin was accented by the cutoff shorts and bikini top she wore. I couldn't figure how she got away with wearing such an outfit in front of her own father.

"She was a lot younger then," I told him.

Crillian turned to her. "Don't know if you remember Aston, either."

"I remember he was a hot-shot pilot with the Gryphon Defense Force. You met us while dad covered joint exercises between the Rulusian Militia and the Gryphon Defense Force."

"Impressive she remembers so much about things so long ago."

"Kid's smart. Must take after her mother."

I wasn't comfortable speaking of the dead, whether good or bad. I never knew his wife, but it didn't matter in my mind.

I moved the conversation on with a chuckle. "Too bad my hot-shot pilot days are behind me."

"I bet you're an excellent pilot." Juniper walked around the table and sat beside me. She sat so close, I felt her body heat and it made me uncomfortable.

Crillian asked, "What are you doing then?"

"Scavenger pirate."

"Don't you think you're qualified for a little more than that?" He stood with a frown and walked toward the kitchen area.

"I started out as a commercial transport pilot, but it was too boring." That being said, even I had my limits on how much excitement I could handle, especially lately.

"What's so boring about it?"

"Never getting to see anything new, flying the same route in my sleep, every trip? Nothing about it spelled excitement to me."

"There's nothing exciting about getting yourself killed." He opened his cupboard and searched.

"Don't mind him. I think it's very exciting." Juniper's dainty green hand came to rest on my leg. Out of reflex, my leg jumped as I watched the lust in her eyes. What was she doing, and with her father in the next room?

I stood and walked to the counter, then stood across from Crillian.

He looked around the open cupboard door and his wrinkled forehead told me he was surprised to see me, but Crillian didn't miss a step as he pulled out three glasses. He smiled at me and set them down. "Now it's time we celebrated this happy reunion."

I heard Juniper stand from the couch behind me just before Crillian drew my full attention. "So, do you remember the last time you were here?"

"Vaguely."

"Do you remember the night we went to Daklar's?"

That night hadn't been one of my finest moments. "The bar?" He nodded, as more memories slipped in. "They had a special drink, what was it called?"

"Jungle Juice." Crillian chuckled under his breath.

Upon hearing the name, it all came back. The drink was made using a pair of Rulusian fruits, which were nothing but plain fruit juice by themselves. When combined in the proper combination, though, the concoction became heavily alcoholic. There were very few liquors which could put me down in low quantities, and Jungle Juice was one. I hadn't had a great time the morning after our first meeting.

"Daklar took our suggestion, bottled it up and sold it in all the markets."

If I remembered right, our suggestion had been made under the influence. "All suggestions sound good to the intoxicated."

"He's making a fortune as we speak."

"Guess we should have joined up with him."

"Probably so. But I still get a few perks." He smiled at me and opened a cooler underneath the counter, before he pulled a tall, dark green bottle out. He attempted to pour a glass, but only a few dribbles fell out of the bottle.

Juniper's voice dripped sarcasm as she told him, "Looks like all those 'little sips' have caught up with you."

I smiled, glad I wouldn't have to decline the offer. Rulusians became upset if you didn't accept their personal gifts, which included glasses of Jungle Juice.

Crillian spoke in a somber tone, "Well, I guess there's only one way to solve this." He looked at each of us, then grinned from ear to ear and gave a hearty laugh. "Go to Daklar's and get some more."

Juniper complained, "Dad, there's other alcohol in the house.

"But no Jungle Juice. Besides, it's time for dinner."

The matter wasn't up for discussion as he left the glasses out on the counter and marched toward the front door. Juniper and I both followed him out into the hallway.

I again admired the scenery as we walked past. "Why's this place so run down?"

"City doesn't want to fund the maintenance anymore."

"They can just decide that?"

"They determined there weren't enough residents to justify the expense."

"How many residents are there?"

"We're one of, I'd say sixteen families. There used to be ten times as many."

"I thought you had serious congestion problems in this town."

"We still do, just not here on the surface." We reached the end of the hall and he pulled open a door to the stairwell. "Now, almost everyone wants to live in subterranean homes. That's where the city spends all of its money."

"Sounds like you're getting a raw deal to me."

The metal grating echoed as we made our way down the stairs. He shrugged. "It's not all bad. We don't have to pay rent or utilities. We just have to deal with the mess."

"So, when did Rulusia start in with underground housing?"

Juniper answered over the racket. "Have you ever heard of the Torians, one of our neighbor systems?"

I pursed my lips. "A little bit. Why?"

"They went through a natural disaster some time back. Because of the extent of our solar cell energy production, we traded excess power with them in return for their expertise in building underground structures. Our government has built non-stop down there ever since, to try and thin out surface congestion."

We reached the last landing and I saw the exit door below.

It was a shame conditions above ground had to suffer in the name of progress. "So, why haven't you moved down below? I'm sure free rent and utilities aren't a necessity for you."

Crillian scoffed, "I wouldn't want to live underground. You'd never get to see the stars or experience the great outdoors. Like this…" He pushed the door open and led us into the sweltering mugginess. At least the shadows of the surrounding buildings offered some relief from direct heat. I had no idea why he thought the planet's surface was so terrific.

Crillian didn't stop, so I held the door for Juniper. She puckered her lips and blew a kiss at me on her way by.

Did I mention how uncomfortable she made me?

We started toward a building directly across a huge courtyard. Bricks in various shades of brown were organized in a giant circle centered between five apartment towers. The restaurant itself was a grand departure from the apartments, being only a two-floor structure. Its ground floor was adorned with colorful lights and signs. A crowd stood and mulled about while they waited for their chance to get inside. Women's voices carried through the air, and I looked up, where barely dressed ladies sat in window wells and called out to the men in the crowd.

Daklar had certainly done well for himself since I'd last seen him.

I took another look at the sea of green. "Looks like there's quite a wait."

Crillian turned with a sly smile, telling me, "We never wait."

He started for an alleyway at the side of the building and led us to an entrance, posted for 'employees only.' He knocked three times and it was opened moments later by a short stubby Rulusian clothed in a perfectly tailored, light-green suit. A smile was plastered to his wide face.

He embraced Crillian in a hug. "My friend."

Crillian smiled. "Good to see you again, Daklar."

He turned to Juniper and kissed her on the cheek. "Darling, lovely as ever."

She returned the kiss on his cheek, before he turned to me, puzzled. "And you, I recognize, but can't place."

He pinched his chin in contemplation, and closed one of his eyes as if to stimulate his thought process. Then, his eyes grew large and he laughed.

"Aston West?" He swapped glances between me and Crillian. "How could I forget one of the two people to make me such a rich man?"

Crillian interrupted our reunion. "We were interested in grabbing some dinner."

"Come inside. No one is using the VIP table this evening." He led us inside and shut the door. We walked through a storage room full of packing crates.

Daklar chuckled as he stepped through the mess. “Who would have thought an alcoholic beverage could lead to such wealth?”

Crillian laughed. “We did.”

“So you did, my friends. Demand has been so great, I just built another new farm to harvest the fruits I need.”

We walked into the kitchen, which was a flurry of activity.

“The last time I had a bottle, I was out cold. Surely everyone can’t desire to be knocked out all the time.”

Crillian laughed. “Life in the capital isn’t as happy as you might think.”

Daklar turned to Crillian, slapped him on the chest and joined in the laughter. “We aren’t politicians after all, are we, old friend?”

I thought of Ba’lor as our host continued, “I don’t concern myself with the minor details. If people want my product, their money is always good.”

We exited out into a vast room of occupied tables. A bar stretched around three walls of the room, while other patrons waited their turn behind a set of ropes. Customers sat around the room, while bartenders hustled behind the bar and waitresses scurried amongst the tables. I felt very awkward being the only alien in this small army of Rulusians.

We made our way to the near corner, where an empty table held up a ‘Reserved’ placard.

Our waitress walked up out of nowhere. As with her co-workers, Daklar purposely accentuated her looks through shirts with wide fronts and short skirts. Her cleavage looked as if it would fall out at any moment, and her long legs went all the way up. She smiled with a wink of one of her light green eyes. “What would you like to have?”

I could think of so many things, but cleared my thoughts. “You have Vladirian liquor?”

"Afraid not, sweetie."

That was extremely disappointing. "Any house specials?"

Daklar laughed. "Jungle Juice, of course."

"Anything else?" I smirked.

"Blasphemy," Crillian scoffed.

The waitress continued, "We have a very nice Barian ale."

"I'll take it."

Crillian grunted. "I can't believe you've finally returned to Rulusia and aren't going to have any Jungle Juice."

"I'd better keep at least partial control of my wits."

"Your loss." He shrugged.

The waitress took everyone else's drink orders, then gave me another wink as she left the table.

Juniper followed her movements with a scowl. "Trashy whore."

I found her comments rather rude, and just about told her so before Daklar jumped in, saying, "She gave that life up, my dear. You shouldn't refer to her as such."

I looked over at him and he laughed. "I guess I should explain. Our waitress worked for the brothel upstairs, but wanted to leave the business, so I asked a favor of my friend in charge up there. He was happy to oblige, after all the business I've brought him."

Juniper wasn't convinced. "She's still a trashy whore. Whether she gets paid for it or not is beside the point."

We fell into silence as the waitress returned with our drinks. She lingered by my side, while she placed a mug of clear liquid in front of me. I breathed in her beauty before she continued around the table.

The last drink was placed in front of Juniper, who shot back an angry stare in return.

Crillian spoke up, "Well, I don't know about the rest of you, but I'm starving. I'll take a Rubuk sandwich with everything."

Juniper and Daklar gave their orders, then the server turned her attention to me. "What can I get you?" Her seductive voice made me sure she had done quite well in her former profession.

"I'm not sure. What do you recommend?"

Her eyes sparkled against the light green background of her face. "For a man like you, I think a Borolo steak, cut from one of the biggest beasts in the jungle."

I turned my attention to the menu. "Sounds expensive."

Daklar announced, "Don't worry about price. This is all covered."

"Borolo steak it is, then." The waitress smiled, tucked her order pad in the front of her skirt, and walked away from the table.

"She has an interest in you, my friend," Crillian noted with a laugh.

I turned and watched her retreat toward the bar, as her hips swayed back and forth. The sweet fragrance of lust still lingered in the air. I shook my head and turned back to the conversation.

"I'll just ponder what might have been." I brought the mug to my lips and the sweet bubbly fluid flowed down my throat.

Daklar raised one of his eyebrows. "Don't you find her attractive?"

"Attractive and tempting." I took another drink. "Unfortunately, she's not my style."

"Since when?" Crillian laughed.

I shrugged, and took another long drink. She wasn't the first to try and use her femininity to her advantage with me, and wouldn't be the last. Talani had been the same way. I wasn't always successful, but tried my best to steer clear of such women.

Crillian scoffed, "And you call yourself a pirate?"

I hoisted my ale high in mock tribute and drank the remainder, then set the empty mug down and made a personal vow to slow down.

Juniper piped in, "Besides, who knows what kind of disease-ridden filth that whore has laid down for?"

"Juniper!" Her father chastised.

Daklar turned to Crillian and thankfully changed the subject, "So, how goes the latest story?"

"As slow as a Hurlabeast in a mud pit. No one wants to be associated with this mess."

"Politicians." Daklar hefted his glass.

They'd touched off my curiosity. "What's this?"

Crillian dipped his head and spoke so soft as to barely be heard, "Rumor has it Toris is on the verge of civil war."

It wouldn't be wise for me to spill what I knew, so let them continue.

"It seems our government leaders secretly shipped weapons to Toris. I don't know which side they want to back, but just the fact they're involved makes for a juicy story."

Juniper rubbed a finger around the rim of her glass. I noticed she hadn't touched a drop of Jungle Juice herself. "Why would anyone want to get involved in someone else's war?" She asked.

"If I knew, I'd already have my story." Crillian drank the rest of his glass. "Unfortunately, the politicians have all become tight-lipped. I've hit a dead end, and don't see another way to break the story."

I was curious. “What would people here think if they knew?”

Conversation ceased for a moment as the waitress returned with refills for Daklar, Crillian, and me.

Daklar chimed in once she left, “I don’t see why they’d want to get involved.”

“Exactly. Why would they want to stir up trouble?” Crillian crinkled his forehead.

There was so much I could tell all of them about what I knew. But even though he was my friend, my knowledge would only make matters worse if it became public. Neither a plot to assassinate the President, nor the Torian massacre on-board a freighter full of illegal weapons, would be well received by the Rulusian public.

“Hopefully you find a way to break the story,” I suggested.

Crillian sighed. “Let’s hope so.”

Our food arrived moments later, and conversation moved on to items of a more personal nature as the crowd grew beyond the ropes.

Chapter Nine

After an evening filled with food, drink, and laughter, we left Daklar to run his restaurant and headed back for the apartment. The two stars had both fallen beneath the horizon and the darkness left it reasonably comfortable as we walked back across the courtyard. Juniper walked ahead of me with a cloth sack of Jungle Juice bottles strapped over the crook of her right arm, while I was stuck with her father draped over my shoulder.

I chided him, "What happened to you? You figure out a way to soak up the alcohol instead of drinking it? You weigh a ton!"

"Come on, muscles," he chided, then rolled into a laughing fit. At least one of us was enjoying himself.

It seemed as though the same maintenance woes that plagued the inside of their apartment building were present outside. Only about half of the lights around the courtyard functioned, which didn't give me much to see by as I walked.

We finally made it to their building. Juniper held the door open and I pulled Crillian inside, then looked up the stairway in despair.

She swung the sack over her shoulder with a smirk. "You need some help? Or would it hurt your image?"

"If you're offering, I'm willing."

She grabbed her father's left arm, and the two of us hoisted him up the staircase. The sack of alcohol swung with every step and bottles clanked against one another. It was still slow, but her assistance made it much easier. I needed to find a way to do more than lounge around during long trips on my ship, because I didn't remember myself being this out-of-shape before.

As if he could read my mind, Crillian looked at me with his eyes glazed over and confirmed, "You need some exercise. Look at the trouble you're having."

I spoke amongst labored breaths, "Yeah, I'll get right on that."

Juniper was almost as out of breath as I was. "We wouldn't be in this mess if you hadn't had so much Jungle Juice."

I shook my head. "How many was it, three, four?"

"Five," Crillian said with a smile.

"Six," his daughter corrected.

"And they were all worth it." He grew solemn and serious, then his head dropped as the sixth bottle took effect and he passed out.

"Amazing he's able to handle so many and still be coherent for so long."

Juniper rolled her eyes. "He's had lots of practice."

"So, how do you usually get him back home?"

"He usually doesn't go out to get this way. Normally, he just passes out on the couch, and I leave him be."

"Lucky."

We pushed our way back into the hallway, and stumbled to their front door. Juniper let her father go, which forced his full weight on me again as she pulled out her set of keys. I kept myself upright as she opened the door, then jogged into the kitchen and dropped off the sack of Jungle Juice.

I figured he'd be better off waking up in his own bed. "Let's get him to his room."

We carried him past the threshold, before Juniper closed the door behind us and instructed, "Down the hall."

I scurried to keep up with her as we started through the narrow corridor. "So, what are your plans?"

"After I leave Rulusia?"

"Yeah," she said.

We walked into his room and the hall light guided us. Flopping him onto the mattress, I stood and watched him a moment. "Think he looks comfortable enough?"

"I'm too worn out to move him if he's not."

"He's comfortable," I confirmed.

I followed her back down the hallway as she continued, "So, you were saying?"

"I have some cargo to unload. I'll probably find some place to do that."

Her eyes sparkled in the dim light when she turned to look. "Something illegal?"

I smiled. "What's a girl like you doing with those kind of smarts?"

"I'm working for the KOMA Institute, have been for a few cycles now." Her face flushed as she looked down at the floor.

"Doesn't seem it makes you too happy. What do you do?"

"Scientific experiments, inventions, and the like. It's so boring, especially the people."

She turned and stretched her arms across the hall, blocking my path. "I'd much rather hang out with someone exciting like you."

"Trust me, my life is far from exciting." I chuckled under my breath.

Except of course, when I have a death penalty hung over my head, or an assassin trying to kill me. Unfortunately, exciting never ended up being a good thing in my life.

"You have to check out my room." Juniper grabbed my hands and drug me through another doorway. She flipped on the light switch and my sight was flooded with hot pink walls.

She released me and I glanced around the room. It was what one would expect of a girl her age, on the fine border between late-adolescence and adulthood. She still had a number of toys, pillows, and knick-knacks from years gone by, mixed in with more adult items, such as bottles of liquor and posters of various artists with questionable musical talent. Clothes and skimpy undergarments were strewn all over.

"So, what do you think?"

I smiled. "Quite nice. Now, I'm going to head out to the couch and try to get some sleep."

"Don't be such a party-pooper. Let's have a little fun." She reached out and grabbed my side. Out of instinct, I flinched again.

"Why do you pull away from me?"

I shrugged.

"You don't find me attractive?"

"You're attractive, trust me." It was true, despite my attempts to convince myself otherwise.

"Then, what's the problem?"

"It's complicated."

Her emotions became a mix of anger and sorrow, a deadly combination for me, being on the receiving end. "But not as attractive as other females. If I was that whore waitress, you wouldn't have a problem with it."

If she'd forced me into her bedroom as Juniper just had, that was likely true.

"It's not the same."

"How so?"

"You're my best friend's daughter."

"And?"

"It would be awkward."

"That shouldn't make any difference."

"The last time I saw you, you were a little girl. Of course it does."

Not to mention Crillian being someone who could break me open like a bottle of Jungle Juice.

"I'm a woman now," she announced with pride. Then, to prove her point, she reached up and yanked her top off in one motion.

"Juniper!" I averted my wide eyes, but the damage to my memory was already done.

"Aston, look at me!"

I gave a nervous laugh. "Um, no?"

"Look at me!" Her tone told me she wasn't going to accept any excuses.

I turned and stared straight into her face. My skin crawled as I remembered Crillian lay in the next room. He would kill me, and I was certain it wouldn't be quick or painless.

She walked over to me and yanked my jacket to the floor, then pressed against my chest. "Now, I find you attractive and I'm certain you feel the same for me. Are you going to let past memories stand in the way?"

I wanted to end this, but didn't know how to respond, so stood there speechless. She preyed on my moment of confusion, reached up to nestle my face with her hand and planted a passionate kiss on the mouth. I didn't stop what was happening, because it felt good. I hadn't had physical contact with a female of any species in a long time. Her assault on my senses continued as she combed her fingers through my hair, and our mouths pressed against one another.

As she reached down to my pants, my conscience slapped me upside the head and I grabbed her arm. "I can't."

"Why not?"

"I'm sorry, I just can't."

She pulled away and folded her arms across her chest. Her cheeks were flushed and her eyes drooped. "Please leave."

"If the circumstances were different, Juniper, I…"

"Leave!" Her eyes burned through me.

I walked out of the room, and the door slammed shut behind me. I looked down the hall toward Crillian's room and listened for signs of my forthcoming death. All I heard were heavy sobs from behind Juniper's door.

It had been the right thing to do, but my heart sank. There had been no good way to get out of what just happened, but now I had to live with the fact I'd just crushed a young woman's feelings of lust for me.

I did have to question her taste, but there would be a time and a place to do so and now was not it.

With a sigh, I walked off into the living room, then second-guessed myself and turned into the kitchen. My mind was running at top speed, and there would be no way I could sleep with the thoughts and images in my head. I needed some help, so grabbed a Jungle Juice bottle from the sack and one of the empty glasses Crillian had left out earlier. I poured a glass and walked over to the couch. I stared at the green liquid for a moment or two, and hoped I'd forget all about what just happened by the next morning. Then, I gulped the entire drink down and set the glass on the table. I reached over to turn off the lamp, but my vision began moving back and forth, then duplicated itself and began to rotate in wide circles. I fell sideways on the couch as my vision went black.

• • •

Loud pops and the greasy smell of fried flesh woke me from my induced slumber. My head felt like it was sandwiched between two cargo containers as I attempted to open my eyes. Tears formed as the pain increased and all the memories of the night before came flooding back. I cringed, knowing that my attempt at a memory wipe had failed.

Crillian called out from somewhere nearby. “Sleep well?”

I cracked my eyelids. “Not really.”

“I figured you might like some more Borolo, as much as you enjoyed it last night.”

Last night hadn’t ended up as terrific as it had started, but I wasn’t about to start down that road with him. I stood and walked gingerly over to a small wall separating the living room from the kitchen. “Thanks.”

“Granted, the server isn’t as attractive.” He winked and shook a skillet filled with a handful of meat strips. “Borolo slices, along with Japali eggs.”

He placed the black pan back over an open flame, then handed me a plate with two eggs resting on one half.

“Looks good.”

He grinned as he pulled three Borolo slices out of the skillet with his fingers and tossed them on my plate. “They’re pretty hot, so let them cool or you’ll burn yourself.” He tossed the other three on a second plate and flipped a wall switch to shut off the flame. The two of us walked back into the living room and sat down on separate couches.

Crillian shoved an egg in his mouth, then stored it in the bulge of his cheek before he spoke, “So, what happened last night? After dinner?”

"Well, we hauled your drunk carcass home to sleep it off." I chewed on a Borolo strip and savored the tender meat with a slight spicy taste.

"I need to cut back. I'm not as young as I used to be."

"I know the feeling."

"If only they didn't make alcohol so tasty." He gave a slight laugh.

I joined in with a chuckle as Crillian continued, "So, what did you and Juniper end up doing last night?"

I surprised myself with how fast I responded. "Not much, talked about jobs and stuff."

I shoved another piece of Borolo in my mouth to delay the conversation.

"Did she try to get in your pants?"

I choked on the meat and had to smack myself on the chest to clear it out.

"You okay?'

My voice was raspy as I tried to buy myself some more time. "Yeah, I'm fine. Just ate too fast."

"So, Juniper? Your pants?"

"Dad!"

I turned with wide eyes at Juniper's voice. There she stood in the arch of the hallway, thin fabric barely concealing her body. Her eyes were red and I hoped she hadn't cried all night long.

"Morning, sweetie."

"Dad, what were you talking about?"

"Nothing, dear." He turned to me and winked.

"I hope not." She turned and stormed back into her room. "I'm going to shower. Try not to turn on the water."

We sat and ate our breakfast as Juniper made a racket in her room, then walked down the hall to shower. Once the door closed behind her, Crillian continued our previous conversation.

"I probably should have warned you before we went out last night. Juniper's reached adulthood and is going through biological changes. I don't want to bore you with the specifics, but one of the side effects is sporadic spikes in sexual desire and territoriality."

"Yeah, that would have been nice to know." I still had no intention of bringing up specific details of the previous evening, and hopefully he would never find out.

"She didn't cause you too much grief, did she?"

"Nothing terrible."

He sighed. "Apparently it's something every Rulusian girl goes through. The doctors say it's just a phase."

"Lucky you."

"I just hope I can hold out that long."

We polished our plates clean and Crillian took them over into the kitchen. He rinsed them off, forgetting his daughter's warning. She screamed from the bathroom.

Crillian cringed, then walked back to the couch. "So, what are your plans?"

"Don't have any yet."

"I'm supposed to research my latest story, but I have this feeling work will have to wait. Perhaps you'd like to go underground."

"Sounds good."

"I'll see if Juniper wants to go with us."

I almost frowned at the notion. I wasn't sure I could handle a trip with Juniper and her father. I would have hoped having him around would restrain her a bit, but wasn't so sure.

He stood and walked down the hallway out of sight. I heard him knock on a door and call out, "Baby, Aston and I plan to head underground. You want to come with?"

I barely made out her response over the sound of rushing water. "Yeah."

Crillian walked back out into the living room. "I guess we'll leave in a little bit. Want some Jungle Juice while we wait?"

"I had some after we got back last night. It treats me the same now as the last time."

"You just don't drink often enough."

I chuckled. "I wouldn't go that far."

Just before he sat down, there was a knock at the door.

I looked over at Crillian. "Expecting company?"

He raised an eyebrow and shook his head. There was another knock and he started toward the door. "I'd better get it."

He walked over and opened the front door slightly. "Can I help you?"

"Are you Crillian Castril?"

"Yes."

"We're looking for Aston West."

Crillian's attitude picked up a notch. "What for?"

"The Rulusian President has requested his presence."

I cut Crillian off before he got himself in trouble. "It's okay."

He looked at me like I was insane, but opened the door for two Rulusians in all-black dress uniforms who walked inside.

"I'm Aston West."

Juniper walked into the room with damp hair. At least she was clothed, albeit in a similarly skimpy outfit to the one she had on the previous night. "What's going on?"

"The President wants to see Aston," Crillian told her.

She looked at me, stunned. "What did you do to get that kind of attention?"

I shrugged. "I wish I knew."

Crillian jumped in. "We'd better come with you."

One of the guards held up his hand. "I'm sorry. Our orders are to bring Mister West."

"They're with me. If they don't go, I'm not going."

He looked back and forth between all of us and pondered his options a moment. "Okay, all of you can come."

It was a good sign. If I was in trouble, my demand would have been shot down. Still, I wasn't sure what was going on, and though that seemed to be a common occurrence anymore, it bothered me.

Chapter Ten

Soon after, we stood in the transport area of the Capitol building, which was pristine compared to Crillian's building. Marble tile was weaved in intricate patterns under our feet while bright light reflected off the pale dome above.

I turned to my friend. "Are you sure they're spending all their money underground?"

He smirked. "All the money they're willing to spend on us lowly common folk."

"A fraction of what they spend on themselves." Juniper frowned.

Ba'lor and Rione walked into the room. This didn't bode well.

The politician smiled. "Everyone, the President is waiting for us. If you would, please, follow me."

He led us through a grand hallway, where portraits of past Presidents looked down upon all who passed. Other politicians, dressed in the same fashion as Ba'lor, sat on benches against the wall. A few stood in pairs.

Most of them spoke with other politicians or finely dressed friends. We were invisible to them all while walking by, being the only ones present beneath the upper crust of society. I would have thought my pale skin an oddity, worthy of at least a sidelong glance.

While we followed our escorts, Crillian spoke in a hushed whisper, "So, what do you think he wants to see you for?"

"I wish I knew."

Juniper smiled. "And here you told me your life wasn't exciting."

I ignored her comment.

A few moments later, we entered a much larger room with a giant domed ceiling. Support pillars were arranged in a large circle, half the size of the room. A beam of light shot up from the center of the room, reflecting off the ceiling tiles.

"Impressive," I noted.

"The Grand Chamber. This is where all legislation is made, then they go into the General Assembly for the formalities." Crillian nodded toward the far wall to the left. An archway stood twice as tall as any of the politicians, with a darkened room beyond.

More politicians walked around the room in small groups. I watched one particular group join another. Heads nodded during the discussion, then they moved as one toward another nearby group to assimilate them as well.

We trekked across the Grand Chamber, before coming to a set of huge wooden doors nestled in a second archway. Each guard grabbed onto a golden ring and tugged the monstrosities open. Ba'lor and Rione walked inside while the rest of us followed.

The next room was a scaled-down version of the Grand Chamber, even down to the domed ceiling. Plate glass windows offered a panoramic view of the city and sunlight brightened the entire room. The President sat in an elaborate sculpted chair behind his giant desk at the far side of the room. A large table jutted out toward us with a dozen chairs arranged on either side. The doors were closed behind us as Ba'lor and Rione took the two seats closest to the Rulusian leader.

The President stood from his chair. "Aston, thank you so much for coming."

"Wasn't by choice."

He came around his desk and walked toward me, then looked at Crillian. "I see you've brought friends." I began to introduce them, but he didn't give me a chance. "Mister Castril, always a pleasure to meet such a persistent reporter."

Crillian responded in an awkward mumble, "Thank you, sir."

"And you must be his beautiful daughter." Juniper blushed as he kissed her hand.

I interrupted, "I hear you wanted to speak with me."

"Yes, I wanted to thank you personally for saving my life." He extended his hand.

"What's this?" Juniper turned toward me, eyes wide.

Crillian slipped me a smile. "Are you keeping things from me?"

The President laughed. "You mean, he didn't tell you? He and my good friend Rione Sc'lari stopped an assassin's plan to kill me." He motioned in her direction.

The friendship between Rione and yet another government official didn't slip past my attention.

"So, I'm friends with a certified hero?" Crillian beamed.

I pursed my lips. "Who needs a hero?"

The President smiled. "Apparently, I do."

"Of all the things not to tell me," Crillian said with a sigh, then turned his attention back to his leader. "Who would want to assassinate you, sir?"

"We've determined the assassin was sent by the Torian government."

"Why would the Torian government want you dead?"

It was fun to watch Crillian bait his trap. It got even better when the Rulusian President fell right in.

"Their motives are unclear at this time."

"Do you think it might have something to do with Rulusia supplying weapons to a planet on the verge of civil war?"

The President stood there in silence, his expression unchanged. He took a moment to ponder his answer. "That was one of many suggestions brought up in closed chambers. As of this moment, Rulusia has never supplied a single weapon to anyone, anywhere."

I blinked hard. How could he blatantly deny it when he knew what I'd witnessed? Granted, most politicians were born liars, but this was an easy fact to call him on.

Crillian tilted his head to the side. "As of this moment?"

"Yes."

My mind made the connection. Rione's shipment had been the first and he merely bent the truth to fit the reality he wanted to portray.

I jumped into the mix. "And what about the future?"

"We have to keep our options open."

Juniper folded her arms across her chest. "Getting involved in other planets' conflicts is actually an option?"

"Every option must be weighed in terms of its pros and cons."

"That's just stupid," she huffed.

He motioned toward the table. "If you'd like, I had planned to discuss the situation on Toris with Ba'lor and Rione when I was told you were on your way. I'd be honored if all of you could join us."

Crillian jumped at the opportunity and took the seat next to Ba'lor. Hesitant, I sat next to Rione while Juniper grabbed the chair beside mine.

The President walked back around and sat down at his desk. "I understand there's been a new development?"

Rione began, "Princess Wren has learned of a new high power satellite station in the final stages of construction. With this satellite, they'll be able to monitor large groups underground."

Ba'lor interrupted, "Which means they'll be able to track the freedom fighters?"

"Easily." She frowned. "They'll be slaughtered once the staging areas are discovered."

Juniper jumped in to the conversation, "They'd kill their own people?"

I frowned. "That's what happens when you rebel against your own government."

The President continued, "You mentioned a new high power satellite?"

"We'd heard that there was work being done on one by the Defense Division." Rione turned to face me. "They improved their transmitter power with blue organic crystals."

My eyes widened and it felt like my heart stopped. It couldn't be a coincidence.

Her eyes burned and her emotion ridges became a deep red color. "And Aston delivered these crystals right into the hands of their Director, Larin Scath."

Everyone looked at me in disbelief.

"I was just hired to make a delivery. How was I supposed to know what those crystals were going to be used for?"

Ba'lor raised an eyebrow. "You should have asked."

"As if they would have told me they were planning to use them to kill people." I still felt sick to my stomach, despite my ignorance.

The President motioned for everyone to settle down. “Now is not the time for arguments or blame. There must be a decision made on how to help these people.”

“Can you send forces to Toris to prevent the killing?” Rione asked.

“Members of the Legislature are working on it at this moment.”

Crillian responded, “Will these ships be used as offensive weapons, sir?”

“No, Mister Castril. They will be used to prevent the Torian government from committing genocide.”

“The Princess has requested that I return to Toris immediately,” Rione interjected.

Ba’lor nodded. “I plan to return with Rione so we have an eyewitness account of the atrocities as they occur.”

“Very good.”

“The only question is how we will get back. Will there be a ship available for me to take?” Rione frowned.

The President rested his elbows on his desk and tented his fingers. “Unfortunately, until a resolution is passed, sending Rulusian ships into Torian territory would lead to bigger issues.”

“We need a way to get there.”

The President turned to me. “Aston, I know you have helped out tremendously up to this point, but I’d like to ask one more favor of you.”

A sinking feeling hit my gut.

“Would it be possible for you to transport Ba’lor and Rione back to Toris?”

I would have laughed in his face at the request, but things weren’t as simple anymore. Knowing I’d been used to help massacre people, I felt obligated. After all my attempts to try and steer clear of this situation, I'd been involved from the beginning without even knowing it.

So, I did the unthinkable. "Okay."

Rione's face was full of shock and surprise, then she jumped on the opportunity. "When do we leave?"

"Better be soon, before I change my mind."

Everyone stood from their chairs, while I sat there. I hoped I was doing the right thing. Juniper leaned down and whispered in my ear, "Glad to see there are still heroes left in this universe."

This wasn't going to go well, I could already tell.

• • •

I was pushed against the restraints one more time as our transport arrived back at the landing pad. Crillian, Juniper and I climbed out onto the platform, while the others piled out of a second transport behind us.

I faced my friend and he gave me another crushing bear hug. "Take care of yourself, okay?"

I attempted to get enough air to speak. "You too."

He took a step back. "Come back soon."

"I will." I just hoped my body could withstand a return trip.

"I expect you to make good on that promise." Juniper walked up to me and gave me a kiss on the cheek, then whispered in my ear, "I'll be waiting for you."

She stepped away and winked at me. I mumbled, "I'm sure."

"Are we prepared to depart?" I turned and Rione was on the other side of me.

"Whenever you are."

"Let's go, then."

I waved to my friends as I walked for the door, Rione at my side and Ba'lor behind us. She told me, "It looks like the kid has a thing for you."

I laughed under my breath. "Childhood crush."

We stepped out into the sweltering sauna and the two of us again became drenched in sweat as we walked over to my ship. I entered my code into the keypad beside the door.

Jeanie's voice carried outside while we waited for the stairway hatch to lower. "Welcome back, Aston. I trust you had a good visit."

"For the most part."

"We have visitors?"

It was time to get down to business, as I climbed up into the ship. "Set in a course back to Toris. We're taking these two back to the orbital station."

"Acknowledged."

I turned to my passengers while they boarded. "Prepare for departure. This won't take long." They nodded while I walked to the bridge.

As I plopped down in my captain's chair, Jeanie announced, "Course is laid in."

"Prepare for takeoff."

The engines came on-line before screens and panels flickered to life. I turned my attention to the communications console. "This is Sierra-Tango-Four-Two-Four, requesting departure clearance."

"Four-Two-Four, this is Traffic Control. Skies are clear, and orbital lanes are empty. You are clear to depart from sector thirty-seven."

"Acknowledged."

"Jeanie, take us out."

We lifted off the pad, before she brought us around to the opposite heading. Once we reached a safe altitude, the main engines lit off and we headed toward the edge of the atmosphere.

Chapter Eleven

I leaned back in my chair as we hit constant velocity and star trails raced around the viewscreen. Hyperspeed travel still amazed some people, but when you'd been through as many trips as I had, it became repetitive and dull, which is where my drinking problem came in. I reached down and grabbed my bottle of Vladirian liquor.

This was lunacy. Nothing good could come from my return to Toris, which is why I'd vowed never to do so. As I swallowed the last remnants of the sweet yellow liquid, Rione entered the bridge behind me.

She crinkled her forehead as she sat down and looked over. "So, why did you agree to help us?"

"Are you complaining? I could just dump you off somewhere if you rather."

"I'm just curious." She watched the viewscreen a few moments. "It just seems out of character for you to get involved without reward or compensation."

"Despite what you may think, I'm no mercenary."

"So, why help out?"

I sat up and looked over. "I feel responsible for what happens to those people."

"So, it makes you feel good to help?"

"I suppose so."

Her smile grew sinister and I knew I'd just given her a weakness to exploit. "Just think how much better you'd feel if you gave them back their weapons."

Why had I said anything? "You told me Rulusia would give you more weapons."

"Until the Legislature approves more direct involvement, no."

"Won't that be soon enough?"

"We don't have that kind of time." Anxiety crept into her voice. "As soon as that satellite station is launched, Torian rebels will get massacred without proper protection."

Deep down, I knew she was right, and my conscience wouldn't allow me to sell my weapons, knowing they could have saved lives.

"Okay, I'll do it. But hurry, before I change my mind." The thought of giving away so many credits was going to hurt for a long time.

Rione was ecstatic as she encouraged me, "We're very thankful. I'm very thankful." She paused while gathering her thoughts. "I need to get word to Lucian."

"Can't transmit until we come out of hyperspeed."

"Let me know when we get close."

She stood and started for the back as I sat silent. Jeanie grabbed my attention after Rione left the bridge. "Why do you feel responsible for what happens to the Torians?"

Another sigh. "Those organic crystals I delivered are being used to help the government commit mass murder."

"So you're giving back the illegal weapons?"

I didn't really need or appreciate any reminder. "Yes."

"I'm sure it's the right thing for you to do." I knew she hadn't wanted me to take the weapons in the first place, so it was silly for her to reassure me.

"Doesn't make it any easier." She kept any further comments to herself as I leaned back in my chair. "Let me know when we arrive."

I barely heard her before my eyes closed. "Acknowledged."

• • •

The remainder of the trip back to Toris was uneventful, which was a pleasant change of pace. Rione was again at my side as we dropped back to normal speed.

"Communication controls are right there," I told her, pointing to the console. With a few keystrokes, she established contact. The left-hand side of the screen reverted to a shot of Princess Wren's head and shoulders.

"Your highness, we have good news. We have the remainder of the original weapons shipment."

The Princess frowned. "Although that's a pleasant surprise, what happened to the plan of a new shipment?"

"The Rulusian legislature has gotten jumpy. Apparently, a reporter has gotten wind of the original plan."

I smiled. In a way, I was glad that Crillian had gotten the story he'd wanted, even if it was one of the reasons I was giving up on a bunch of money.

"Have the Rulusians cut off all support, then?"

"They're currently working up a resolution to offer help."

"At least that's something." She furrowed her brow. "I'll contact Malone and let him know you're on the way."

"We just need a destination."

Wren looked off-screen a moment. "We can receive you in hangar two."

"What's the latest from the planet?"

"It appears a launch is imminent."

"So we're going to be too late?" Rione bit her lower lip.

"To stop the launch, yes. But we can still prevent my father from committing mass murder, if we arm the rebels before he tracks them down."

"We've also run into another issue."

"What's this?"

"The ambassador was an assassin sent by the Torian government to kill the Rulusian President. She tried to murder us during the trip."

"It appears the conflict has progressed beyond an internal affair. I'll step up security on the station. We'll watch for you." Without another word, she terminated the transmission.

Rione turned to me, her emotion ridges were a light shade of violet. "I just hope we don't end up being too late."

"I'm sure it'll be fine.

I placed my hands behind my head. "Jeanie, are there any ships out there?"

Jeanie didn't hesitate. "Negative." At least I wouldn't have to worry about an ambush by Torian cruisers.

We watched in silence for a while, and the station drew closer until Rione broke in, "I just want to thank you again for what you're doing."

"Let's hope it's enough."

"A ship has left the planet's surface," Jeanie alerted us.

The hairs on the back of my neck rose. "Identify."

"It appears to be a small transport."

Rione smiled beside me, while her emotion ridges turned light pink. "Malone."

I drew a deep breath. "Anyone else, Jeanie?"

"Negative."

I was surprised, but had no time to dwell on it as a message came through from the station. "Welcome back, Sierra-Tango-Four-Two-Four. You are cleared for arrival in hangar two."

"Acknowledged." Docking lights flashed on top of the hub, and Jeanie took us in. I unstrapped my holster and tucked it into my side pocket next to the bottle.

It wasn't long before Ba'lor, Rione, and I stood on the hangar floor next to my ship. A pair of sliding doors opened along the wall to our right, as Wren and three armed guards walked in.

"Malone should be here shortly."

Rione nodded. "We saw him."

Wren turned to Ba'lor. "Minister, it's good to see you again. I hope we can count on Rulusia's assistance in this matter."

"Unfortunately, many legislators will be worried about the fallout of being associated with shipping illegal weapons into a potential war zone."

"But the rebels…"

"Until the public is convinced of the atrocities your father is committing, I wouldn't count on much."

"Speaking of which…" Wren turned back to me. "I assume the weapons are ready for transfer?" I nodded, glad her demeanor toward me was more civilized than when we last spoke.

I pulled the transmitter off my belt. "Jeanie, open the cargo bays and bring out the containers."

The hinge motors echoed a slow, dull whine inside the cavernous chamber. I looked around at the rest of the hangar, seeing two military fighters, Adelphi Industries AI-3's, in a dark corner. Those brought back memories of my time as the hot-shot fighter pilot Juniper had remembered. I chuckled under my breath.

Lucian turned for the door. "We can wait for Malone in my office. It's a little more comfortable."

Anything had to be better than standing around in a cold, dreary hangar, so we followed her back through the double doors.

Rushing along a small, elevated circular walkway, I looked over the railing and saw the commons area far below. I hadn't even known this area was up here when I'd first visited the station, and neither did other travelers, so it seemed. Our group continued on to another set of sliding double doors on the far side of the walkway. Rione, Ba'lor and I followed Wren in and her guards waited on the walkway as the doors closed behind us.

Her office was much smaller than the Rulusian President's. A few small circular windows looked out on the dark, starry expanse beyond. The only furniture in the room was her desk and a couple more chairs on the other side. I stood to the side, while the three of them sat down.

I now had a vested interest in what was happening. "So, what's the plan?"

Wren looked up at me. "Once your ship is unloaded, you are free to leave whenever you wish."

I tried not to take exception to the dismissal. "And what are the rest of you going to do?"

Rione jumped in. "Transport the weapons to the surface and distribute them to the rebel forces. It won't be enough for everyone, but it should be a healthy start until more weapons arrive."

"Actually, I should check with the President and see if there's been any update on that end." Ba'lor stood from his chair.

He started for the doors, so I went ahead and took his seat. As the doors opened, I heard him speak. "Good to see you again, Malone."

I turned in my chair to look. A pale-faced, blue-eyed man with a square jaw and blonde stubble on top of his head entered with not a word to the Rulusian politician.

I liked him already.

Rione jumped from her chair and ran to him. They embraced and whispered to each other, and I felt a slight jolt of disappointment which faded quickly.

"I trust the trip went smooth?" Wren asked him.

"As smooth as an outdated transport can be." He walked over to the desk with Rione at his side.

He caught sight of me as he neared. "So, I guess you were the one who saved Rione from destruction?"

"It would seem so."

He extended his hand and we shook. "Thanks. I owe you one."

"No problem."

He turned back to the Princess. "It looks like they were ready to load the cargo as soon as I landed."

She turned to me. "It appears you're free and clear, Mister West."

And just like that, my involvement was complete.

A message came in through a small speaker in the corner of the Princess' desk. "Your highness, we're detecting a heavy cruiser in route from the planet."

"Have they made contact?"

"Negative."

"Sound the alarms."

A klaxon erupted around us, while red lights flashed along the walls.

She turned her attention back to us. "It appears the war has begun."

"We aren't going to stand a chance here on this station, not against a heavy cruiser." Malone scowled.

I thought back. "Do you have more warcraft? I saw a pair of fighters earlier."

Wren's face drooped. "Those are all we have. And we have no pilots trained."

Rione was frantic as she turned to me. "You flown combat?"

"Yeah."

"Adelphi?"

I nodded.

"It looks like we need your help again." She grabbed my arm and pulled me out of the room. I had no time to think and could do nothing but follow.

Chapter Twelve

Containers of weapons were stacked in between my ship and the transport as we raced into the empty hangar.

Rione yelled between breaths, "Hurry!"

The AI-3's we ran toward had been the same fighters I'd flown in the Gryphon Defense Force. With narrow bodies, wide wings and a cruciform tail, they were originally designed for atmospheric flight, but were later outfitted with a multitude of embedded thrusters for use in the vacuum of space.

Adelphi was a fairly widespread company, and sold to anyone who had enough money to spend. It astonished me there were only two fighters to defend an entire station, but it was likely they hadn't had enough money for more. From the looks of them, they'd sat around unused for a long while.

"You take the right, I'll take the left," Rione called out.

We separated and bolted for the fighters. I climbed up a ladder and stepped down into the cockpit, then pushed the stairs away. They hit the floor with a clang, just as I shut the canopy and the pressure seal activated.

I looked around the fighter's cockpit to get my bearings, as it had been a while since I'd seen the inside of one. With a quick move, I grabbed the helmet from the forward glareshield and strapped it on. It brought back memories of interceptor patrols on the interstellar traffic lanes around Gryphon.

I hadn't really missed the cramped conditions or the lack of any kind of pressure suit to back up the canopy. Unfortunately, the cockpit was so tight, an additional suit would make it impossible to fly.

I flipped a pair of switches at the forward end of the left armrest and the ion accelerators whirred to life behind me. The underbelly exhaust vents levitated the craft off the ground and I looked over at Rione. Our helmets tuned themselves to the same communications channel, which was indicated by a single tone in my ears.

I lowered the boom microphone which hung off the helmet. "Are we ready?"

"I notified Wren." Rione's fighter levitated off the ground.

As soon as she said it, a klaxon sounded inside the room, mostly muted by the time it passed through my canopy and helmet. A moment later, the massive bay doors in the ceiling began to open outward. Rione took the lead, and moved her fighter away from the wall, out toward the center of the floor. Her exhaust vents scattered plumes of dust as she rose from the floor.

I placed my left hand on the throttle and pushed it gently forward, as I renewed my feel for the controls. The stick on the right armrest was stiffer than I liked, but there wasn't an opportunity to be picky. I moved toward the center of the hangar as Rione passed through the opening above. Then, I thumbed a big black switch on the inboard side of the throttle levers. My lower vents opened in response, and propelled my ship upward. The other fighter waited for me as I passed into the darkness.

"Ready?"

My eyes adjusted to the darkness as I closed the vents. "As I'll ever be."

I slammed the throttles and accelerated toward the planet as Rione stayed right beside me. The exhilaration I felt was unbelievable. It had definitely been a long time since I'd been at the controls of something this powerful.

I still had concerns. "Have we decided how we're going to do this?"

"Stop them, any way we can."

I assumed she knew these were light interceptors. With only one rotary weapons launcher, they wouldn't have much firepower. I didn't know how we were going to stop anyone by ourselves. I looked at the weapons bay panel in the upper right corner of the display, which indicated two short-range missiles. So, not only was I running with a fighter incapable of the task, I was only half-stocked with weapons.

"Have you checked your weapons bay?" I asked.

"Two short-range missiles."

"I have two more. Hopefully four will be enough."

"It will be."

At least one of us was confident.

Just then, two short beeps in my ears notified me of a new contact on the scanner. I looked down at the center of the instrument panel and cycled the target onto the display. A graphical depiction of our foe came up on the target acquisition computer, the TAC, to the left of the scanner. This heavy cruiser was about twice the size of those I'd seen destroy Rione's ship. These were the kind used for bombardment and I didn't figure they were coming to the station to talk. We were still a few moments out of weapons range.

My old instincts took over. "Get in behind the cruiser. We'll be safe from their cannons back there."

"Acknowledged."

I grabbed the control stick tight and eased it far to the right. The fighter banked the same direction and thrusters vectored me into a turn. I watched the cruiser's image circle around the scanner. It passed into the lower left quadrant and I flipped the stick back to the left, coming back around until I saw the tail end of the cruiser through the canopy. Its engine pods were three white-hot globes from my viewpoint a few kilpars away.

Rione came up on my right side as she completed the same maneuver. I looked over and spoke, "When we get in range, put an SRM into the engines. We might not be able to destroy it, but we can try to stop it before it reaches the station."

"Affirmative."

"Mister West?" A pale, blue-eyed face popped up on the external communications screen above the TAC. The face itself was unfamiliar to me, but there was no mistaking his voice.

Larin Scath.

He looked older than I had pictured, with a head which had gone bald long ago. Deep creases and lines ran along his face, while his eyes were sunken into his face.

"The one and only." I wanted to shove my missiles down his throat personally. It wasn't every person in the galaxy who hired an assassin to kill you.

"Mister West, it seems disposing of you is harder than it appears. How very annoying."

"Sorry to disappoint you," I told him.

"Sooner or later, your luck will run out." He nodded off-camera.

"Not now."

"We'll see." He mustered a sinister grin as the screen went blank.

I heard a flurry of tones in my ear, and looked down to see four other craft emerge from the shadow of the cruiser's signature. I smacked myself for not anticipating a tactic I'd used myself more than a number of times, of using the larger vessel to hide your presence. I cycled to one of the targets and the TAC shortly came up with a visual depiction, AI-7's.

Unlike our own, these fighters were multi-use, able to be set up in a number of different configurations, and designed primarily for space combat.

It didn't help my queasiness knowing we now had four weapons for five targets.

I checked the sensors again. "We're almost in missile range."

"Too long to wait. Follow my lead."

I turned to watch as an SRM ejected from the belly of her ship and lit off.

I exclaimed. "We're not in range yet! What are you doing?"

"Just do it," she demanded.

Unsure of her intentions, I fired off one of my own. Compressed air tanks pushed the missile clear of my hull and it fired off blindly. The rotary launcher rotated into the next position and the indicator updated accordingly. Only one left.

"Would you mind telling me…?"

"Get ready to lock on a target in three, two, one, now!"

I moved my hand down to the TAC, and locked the fighter I already had selected. The target was marked with a solid red triangle and moments later, I saw a dashed version appear on the display around Rione's choice. The missiles altered course, homed in on our targets, and the warheads exploded the two fighters into nothing but space dust.

The other two fighters broke formation as the weapons destroyed their compatriots. I took off after the one closest to me.

"We have to stop the cruiser." I looked back as Rione continued toward the cruiser.

The other enemy fighter swept around behind her. I cursed under my breath and turned back to assist her. I watched my scanner as Rione targeted the cruiser. Another SRM ejected from her ship and launched toward the cruiser.

Four missiles might have had a chance, but one wouldn't even have a chance to slow it down enough to matter. A large blue globe of light shot from the fighter behind Rione and struck her fuselage. Even from my vantage point, her interior lights flickered, then extinguished. Her missile streaked past the cruiser, useless as her guidance computer shut off along with the rest of her electronics. At least she had backup life support systems on-board.

I cycled my TAC, locked onto the fighter, and let loose my remaining missile. We were at close range, so its destruction was quick. I relaxed and pulled back on the throttle as I approached the debris field, when a blue flash passed in front of my ship.

I had forgotten the fourth fighter, but he hadn't done the same for me. I flipped the control stick to the left and advanced my throttle. He followed, without the knowledge I was now out of ammunition. I weaved in an erratic pattern to disrupt the fighter's aim, as I didn't need to become another electrical disrupter victim.

Scath's face popped up again. "It appears your demise is imminent, as with your friends on-board the station."

I smirked. "Don't count me out just yet."

"It's only a matter of time."

I switched frequencies to shut him up and tried to come up with a plan. I had no way to destroy the fighter on my tail. Worse, I couldn't stop the cruiser! The station was on the verge of being destroyed and there was nothing I could do.

Lights on either side of the panel flashed yellow, then turned solid as a target lock was established on my fighter. Then the lights turned bright red as a weapon was fired. I watched the scanner as it tracked the weapon's path toward my fighter. The TAC identified it as a heavy torpedo, used for bringing down heavy objects.

Like space stations, I thought grimly.

The fourth fighter turned and bolted for the planet. A torpedo had to be its only armament, which explained why they wanted to disable us with their electrical disrupters first.

I looked back at the TAC as sweat dripped off my face. Then I saw the torpedo's tracking type tucked amidst various detail information. I adjusted course straight for the cruiser and slammed my throttles to full. I watched the massive engines grow larger with every heartbeat and kept a close eye on the closing distance.

The communications screen popped up again with Scath's face, scowling. Apparently he'd found my new frequency. "Are you still here, Mister West? Don't you ever give up?"

I smiled. "Never."

Almost breaking the control stick off in my hand, I flipped the fighter over and skimmed the cruiser's belly at a whisker's distance. Then I pulled back on the stick and did everything short of getting out and pushing to run away from the cruiser. The torpedo destined for my death tracked in on the huge heat sources provided by the massive engines and I smiled as the cruiser exploded behind me.

Chapter Thirteen

A team of four Torians in pressure suits flung ropes over the body of Rione's dead fighter, and guided her down to the hangar floor before I released my tow hook. My landing skids hit solid metal as I touched down a few moments later. The bay doors closed above our heads, and I opened my canopy as soon as the team removed their helmets, indicating that I'd be able to breathe outside.

A ladder was placed against the side of my fighter and I climbed down while the doorway to the corridor slid open. Malone and the Princess started into the room with a pair of escorts. Rione ran around the nose of my fighter and embraced me in a wonderful hug. It was a lot better than being at each other's throats as we had been for so long.

"That was great." She released me. "We could use pilots like you."

"I'm afraid my hero days are behind me."

She was disappointed, but smiled as Malone walked over and embraced her with a kiss. They finished with each other and he turned to me. "That was impressive out there."

I downplayed the situation. "Blind luck."

"Hardly," scoffed Rione.

Wren was ecstatic. "That was superb. It should serve as a fine warning to my father."

Malone's jubilant attitude came to an end. "Princess, the weapons are all loaded. We should get them to the surface."

"Agreed."

He started toward his ship while the rest of us watched.

Rione frowned. "I still can't figure out who leaked the information on the first shipment."

"I'm afraid that would have been me."

We looked around and Ba'lor stood in the open doorway, an automatic burst rifle aimed in our direction.

Rione stared in disbelief. "What is this? What are you doing?"

"Stopping this rebellion before it begins. Now, everyone gather over there." He motioned with the barrel. With the ability to fire continuous shots over a long duration, he could take all of us out easily.

"You won't get away with this," I chastised.

"Won't I?"

Wren gave him a hard stare. "The Rulusian President will hear about this, rest assured."

"It won't much matter, as it will be too late for you and your friends on the planet. Once I deliver these weapons to your father, it will eliminate any chance your insurrection has."

"But why?" Rione whined.

"We have no reason to get involved," he said. I watched as he spoke, while his hands gripped the weapon tightly.

I'd gone through a lot to get the weapons to the rebels, and wasn't too pleased my efforts would be ruined this late in the game.

Malone grunted at the politician. "By stopping these weapons from being delivered, you're still getting involved. Besides, the government is already killing us!" I looked over at him and my eyes drifted down at the holster on his leg.

"If you did what they asked, thought like they wanted you to, there would be no problem."

I looked back at the Rulusian as Malone barked, "They have no right to tell us how to think."

"No matter. This transport isn't going to make it to your compatriots."

I pondered his words and something didn't make sense. "Cut the charade, Ka'lor."

He looked over, puzzled.

"What do you care whether your government sides with the rebels or stays out of it completely? You'll still have the easy life back on Rulusia either way."

He chuckled to himself. "You're right, of course. Torians killing each other doesn't concern me."

"Then why get involved yourself, when you claim Rulusia has no reason to do the same?"

He pondered a moment, then answered with a smirk. "You might say I have a vested interest in the actions of the Torian government. It's too bad you delayed their plan.

I finally put two and two together. "You were in on the assassination attempt…"

"Why?" Wren exclaimed.

Rione complained, "How could you do such a thing?"

"With the President out of the way, I would have no trouble thrusting myself into the Presidency. There would be a special vote of the Legislature, and my victory was assured by the Torian government."

Wren scrunched her pale eyebrows. "Why would we get involved in Rulusian politics?"

Ba'lor dripped with sarcasm. "Why would we get involved in Torian politics?"

A moment of brilliance flashed in my head. "You're trading favors."

He smiled. "Very good, Mister West. I sabotage efforts to help the rebels, and the Torians help me ascend to the Presidency."

A message came through a set of speakers nearby. "Your highness, a pair of Rulusian destroyers have just entered Torian space."

Wren smirked. "Looks like your plan just fell apart, Minister."

"Hardly." He chuckled. "I'm merely going on a diplomatic mission to the surface, to try and stop this conflict."

He sidestepped toward the transport, keeping the rifle trained on us. He drew close to the hull and reached for the hatch release, but couldn't quite find it. Frustrated, he turned his head to look.

I seized the moment, dove to the floor, and grabbed the laser pistol off Malone's calf. Ba'lor turned as I hit the floor with a thud and he lifted the rifle. I pulled the trigger without hesitation. The shrill pitch of the green energy beam echoed through the chamber on its way to my target.

He slammed against the ship, then collapsed to the floor. A pair of guards ran over and kicked the rifle away, then knelt down to check him.

The one closest to us called out, "He's still alive."

I rolled over on my back and exhaled the breath I'd been holding.

Wren spat her words. "Throw him in a holding cell."

Malone reached down to grab my arm. "Good thing I never leave my blaster on the highest setting." He pulled me to my feet as the guards hauled the Minister's limp body out of the hangar.

Rione looked over. “Are you sure you don’t want to stay? We could definitely use you.”

I came out of my state of shock with the aid of a few deep cleansing breaths. “I don’t imagine I could handle much more of this.” I gave a weak smile.

“So what’s next for you?”

“A vacation, I think. This hero stuff is tiring work.”

“And where will you go?”

I shrugged. “Don’t know, but I’ll figure it out when I get there.”

She embraced me in a hug once again, as her ridges turned light pink beside my face. “Take care of yourself, fly boy.”

I chuckled as she let loose and I offered my hand to Malone. “Take care of her.”

He nodded with a smile.

And finally, I turned to the Princess. We stood there in silence for a long time before she finally spoke. “Aston, we’re forever in your debt. If ever you need anything, don’t hesitate to contact us.”

“Thanks, Princess.”

“Please, call me Lucian. All my friends do.” She accentuated her beauty with a smile.

I turned and started toward my ship as Malone walked beside me on his way to the transport. “You know, Rione’s right. We could use the help.”

“I’d like to keep myself in one piece for as long as possible.”

“Understandable.” He smirked. “If you ever change your mind, you know where to find us.”

I hesitated to tell myself I’d never return, because I’d done that once before and remembered how that had turned out. We split up and climbed into our ships.

Jeanie was waiting for me as I climbed inside. “Aston, are you okay?”

“Fine now.”

“I was worried.”

I smiled again at the thought of a machine with feelings. “Nothing to worry about, Jeanie.”

“Can we leave this place?” She asked.

“Prepare for departure.”

The doorway stairs closed behind me and the lights grew brighter. “Do we have a destination?”

I chuckled under my breath as I walked toward the bridge. “Surprise me.”

I sat down in my chair, re-attached my holster and pulled out my bottle. Toris would soon be behind me, and my only hope was another adventure would be a long time coming.

Thank you for reading *Heroes Die Young*. Please enjoy this bonus excerpt, from Aston West's next novel in the series,

Friends in Deed

In the depth of my nightmares, Lycus IV would always be a formidable hell, no matter if the scenery gave off the illusion of mighty grandeur. Lush green trees lined the banks. Sporadic cloud cover offered broken views of a distant pale blue mountain range.

This prison planet's terror was not found in its natural surroundings, but from its unwilling inhabitants.

A wide river flowed slowly before me over a bed of rocks. Filthy clothing, ripped and shredded, barely covered my bruised and bloody skin. I gazed across the clear, inviting water.

A bellow filled the air. I turned as a pale, naked giant rumbled through the brush, yelling at the top of his lungs. His makeshift mallet towered above his head, a boulder strapped into the fork of a tree branch. I jumped aside just before the weapon crashed down.

One of his eyes grew crazy-wide, while the other glazed over. Saliva dribbled from his lips. "I am King of the Wooded Realm! You dare invade my territory?"

This wasn't a fight I planned to stick around for. This beast was obviously psychotic, and they were always the worst type of violent.

He hoisted his club and swung it. I stumbled back and it sent a breeze across my face. Escape was my only chance for survival, so I turned toward the opposite bank and sprinted across the riverbed.

"Your punishment is death! Vengeance is demanded!"

I high-stepped through the water while the beast screamed bloody murder. I didn't want to look back, because that would leave no doubt he gained on me.

My foot tripped over a cluster of submerged rocks and I splashed into the cool, clear water. I flipped over and faced my attacker as his cold, dark shadow enveloped me. Milky-white foam oozed over his lower lip, dripping long strands toward the water below.

"Prepare to meet your maker!"

He raised the mallet high above his head. At least my death would be quick, but I couldn't say much for painless. I shut my eyes tight and waited for the crushing blow.

A sharp whistle passed overhead and the giant beast gasped and choked. My eyes flashed open as the beast dropped his weapon into the river behind him.

Only one object stood between me and oblivion, a homemade arrow buried in his neck, with feathers fashioned into rear fins. He couldn't pull it out from the front, so reached back. The beast's mind finally gave up hope as soon as his fingers felt a stone tip emerging from the back of his neck. His eyes rolled up into his skull, then he fell backward.

The corpse splashed down and huge waves pushed against me. I jerked my head around and stared at the opposite bank. There, a bow in his left hand and a quiver of arrows strapped to his back, stood the man who'd just saved my life.

Elijah Cassus.

• • •

I shot awake, drenched in sweat and breathing heavy. The ship was rapidly decelerating, and something was definitely wrong. My ship's computer usually gave me advance notice before we dropped below the hyperspeed threshold.

I wiped my forehead and tossed my legs over the cot's side, speaking to my computer. "Jeanie, where are we?"

Her seductive voice was little comfort to me. "The Bacauri system."

I involuntarily shuddered, even knowing we'd pass this way when we first set a course for the Tranon system. Quite likely, it was why I'd had a nightmare about my time on Lycus IV. Trouble was, we weren't scheduled to make a stop before reaching Tranon. I scrambled for the bridge. "Why are we slowing down?"

"A power fluctuation interrupted the hyperspeed engines."

This had never happened to me before. But as always, my life was a textbook example of bad timing.

"Once they cool down, continue course."

I slumped into my captain's chair, staring blankly at the viewscreen. A lone red planet, uninhabited, rested several megpars ahead, surrounded by tiny light specks.

I examined the sensor screen in my left side console, and confirmed I wasn't just a victim of overactive paranoia. Sure enough, the Lycus system border was only two megpars off my port side.

I shivered. "Jeanie, how much longer?"

"Should only be a few more moments."

I took a deep, calming breath. The prison planet Lycus IV had driven fear into my heart. My escape definitely hadn't made me any friends with the territorial rulers, the Gohr. It had almost led to my death, more times than I wanted to remember.

Without warning, the viewscreen filled with bright white light. I held my hand up to shield my eyes.

"Incoming transmission, unidentified vessel."

Ships didn't make unscheduled stops in the middle of nowhere, especially when there wasn't a communication beacon anywhere nearby. It meant one thing.

Someone was after me.

"Put it through." A window popped up along the left half of my viewscreen, and I was face-to-face with a Wasirian in a chair. The squat translucent beast stabilized the gigantic bulb, which served as both his upper torso and head, using several hundred short tentacles grasping onto every surface nearby. Black eyes were huge against his green skin.

Wasirians were a nasty species, known for their short tempers and violent tendencies. At least the males. I never knew anyone who'd actually ever met a female Wasirian. It made one wonder if there was a reason they were always so frustrated with the universe.

The beast's tiny beak at the center of his body flapped rapidly. "Give me back my cargo!"

"What cargo?"

"Are you Aston West?"

"Yes, but what..."

One of his tentacles broke from the pack and jabbed at the screen. "Then give me back my Nomarian ale."

I scowled. "I'm telling you, I don't know..."

His forked tongue flapped out from his beak and he hissed and shrieked, loud and shrill, to silence me, before going back to his demands. "You stole my cargo!" His giant bulb doubled in size and deepened to a red color.

I rushed to prevent another interruption. "I didn't steal anything. What proof do you have?"

"An eyewitness saw you do it."

"Then your eyewitness is a liar."

His eyes narrowed to vertical slits. "Give it back or else!"

I muted the audio and spoke to Jeanie. "What's his armament?"

"Proton cannons and a set of four AIR-3's."

Adilphi Interceptor Rockets. I could evade one, maybe two

at the most. Four would be a stretch.

On the other half of my viewscreen, I watched his ship drift, pointed in roughly the same direction as I was. No more than half a kilpar long, the bullet-shaped front transitioned to a rectangular cabin, accented at the rear with four exhaust nozzles. Delta wings were nestled underneath his aft cabin.

His head grew a darker shade of red as I returned to the conversation. "Listen, I'm sorry you lost a shipment of Nomarian ale, but I don't have it. Scan my hold for yourself."

I didn't even know what Nomarian ale looked like, but knew all my holds were empty.

His tongue flapped a few more times. "Everyone knows scans can be deceived!"

True enough, but I didn't have his ale. I wished I did. Business had dried up lately, no pun intended.

"Maybe we can retrace your steps and figure this out."

I had no idea why the idea of using diplomacy even entered my head. It wouldn't have been any use with a Wasirian, even if I'd been good at it in the first place.

"You will not return my ale?" His eyes widened. "Then you will die!"

My life's never dull.

The sub-window disappeared from the viewscreen, which left me an expansive view of the starscape outside.

A skin panel rose along the top of his ship, just forward of the nozzles. His thrusters flashed and the vessel turned toward me. He was about to do something very stupid.

Jeanie confirmed it. "His rocket launchers are deployed and targeting is on-line."

"Idiot." I grabbed the control stick on my left and rested my other hand on the thruster control panel.

The ship banked and propelled itself in response as I

jerked the stick forward and to the left, keeping him from getting a targeting lock. I kept his ship centered in my viewscreen.

"Can you hack into his computer and disable his targeting computer?"

"Negative. I have attempted to do so since he dropped out of hyperspace. He has a very impressive security system in place."

"Guess we'll have to do this the hard way. Bring up the proton cannons, continuous burst."

"Done."

"Disable his targeting computer. Maximum power." The sooner I disabled his ability to kill me, the better.

"Maximum power," she repeated.

I leveled my ship out. "Fire!"

Green beams pulsed from either side of the viewscreen and impaled his launcher.

"Whoa! Cease fire!"

Jeanie obeyed immediately, and the beams dissipated to nothing.

"I wanted to disable his targeting computer, not destroy his warheads."

"His targeting computer is located inside his launch bay. It has been disabled as you requested."

At least no further damage had been done.

Or so I thought, just before all four warheads glowed bright red and then exploded. Another blast followed when debris ripped into the engine pods, and the ship was shredded to pieces. A fireball ignited, then extinguished itself in the vacuum of space. Scrap metal raced away from the scene of the crime. Small fragments pelted my ship and I cringed. The last thing I needed was a hole in my hull. Emergency depressurization in the middle of nowhere would be yet one more nightmare I could live without.

"No life signs detected."

As if there had been any doubt.

I closed my eyes. I hadn't meant for the fool to die. Sure, he hadn't been the first person I'd ever killed, but there was usually a reason someone had to die. Stupidity wasn't one of the better ones.

Why hadn't he just believed me? Now he was dead, because of lost cargo neither one of us had possession of. The truly sad part was neither of us had the ale.

"Wait for the debris field to clear. Then get us out of here."

"Acknowledged."

This brief interruption had given me a respite from my earlier fear. Without death staring me in the face, though, I returned to my thoughts of Lycus IV.

I closed my eyes and took another deep breath. As long as I stayed on this side of the border, I had nothing to worry about. The Gohr were notoriously mean and vicious, a fact to which anyone who'd heard of them could attest. They only left their territory to annex others, though, and for nothing else.

I opened my eyes once again. The sound of debris bouncing off the hull had ceased, yet we hadn't moved. "Jeanie..."

"Forward coolant injectors are not responding." Without coolant, the hyperspeed engines would turn my ship into a ball of liquid metal.

Definitely not anything to experience firsthand.

"Wonderful!" I leaned back and stared at the beige overhead liner, then rubbed my temples. "Can anything else go wrong?"

"I'm picking up a Gohr destroyer departing orbit around the planet."

I double-checked the sensor screen. "What's it doing outside of Gohr territory?"

"I don't have an answer to that."

I turned to the viewscreen. The destroyer rapidly approached and triple-barrel turrets atop the vessel emerged in exquisite detail. Twin stacks were mounted just forward of a raised bridge. One shot, and there wouldn't even be debris left to sift through for my remains.

If they discovered who I was, and they would, my escape from Lycus IV would mean my death. My stomach churned with the knowledge my weapons and hull would be useless against a warship. There was no way I'd outrun them, either, not without operational hyperspeed engines.

"They're closing to weapons range." Jeanie announced. "Incoming transmission."

About the Author

T. M. Hunter has always held a fascination with aircraft and space travel, ending up with a degree in Aerospace Engineering from the University of Kansas. When not designing aircraft, he spends his time designing an entire universe centered around his space pirate Aston West. His short stories have appeared in publications such as *Ray Gun Revival*, *Residential Aliens, Lorelei Signal* and *Golden Visions Magazine* and in both the Aston West collection *Dead or Alive* and the space opera anthology *Raygun Chronicles: Space Opera for a New Age*. He currently has three novels in the Aston West series: *Heroes Die Young*, *Friends in Deed*, and *Death Brings Victory*. And beyond the tales of Aston West, he has also penned the science fiction thriller *The Cure*.

Learn more about the works of T. M. Hunter, read excerpts and stories, and find out his latest news at AstonWest.com. You can also follow him on Twitter (@astonwest) as well as his Facebook fan page (The Aston West Universe).